I0764290

Also by Edward Ronny Arnold

Rebecca

The Lepers

Rashida

The Ram of God

The Tenth Scroll

La Ley del Reemplazo
the Law of Replacement

Plato's Dream

George's Flag

The Harvesting of Joseph Victorio

Published by
Computer Classics ®
Nashville, Tennessee

This is a work of fiction. Names, characters, places, and incidents are used fictitiously. Any resemblance to actual persons, living or dead, events, or locales is entirely coincidental.

The Harvesting of Joseph Victorio
is published in e-book format by
Computer Classics ®
www.computer-classics.com.

ALL RIGHTS RESERVED

Copyright © 2010
Edward Ronny Arnold

Computer Classics ® is a registered Federal Trademark

All rights reserved. No part of this book may be reproduced or transmitted in any form or by any mean, electronic or mechanical, including photocopying, recording, or by any information storage and retrieval system, without the written permission of the Publisher, except where prohibited by law.

ISBN: 9780974887050
LCCN: 2009911451

FACT

The United States Senate created the position of Doorkeeper on April 7, 1789. This position empowered James T. Mathers to ensure senators remained in the Senate Chamber to start the business of government.

The title and duties have changed since 1789. The current title is "Sergeant at Arms and Doorkeeper". The Sergeant at Arms serves the United States Senate as its chief law enforcement officer. Among various duties, the Sergeant at Arms protects the members of the Senate and can arrest or detain any person who violates Senate rules. This power to arrest includes the president of the United States.

With the legal authority to specifically arrest the president, on the orders of the Senate, the "Sergeant at Arms and Doorkeeper" is the most powerful government position that is appointed not elected.

RUMOR

During the War of 1812, as British soldiers advanced on the city of Washington, the populace fled the city. Leesburg, Virginia was a temporary location of the United States government and all of its archives, including the Declaration of Independence and the United States Constitution. A group of people named the Sons of Liberty hid guns, ammunition and an original signed copy of the Declaration of Independence, an original copy of the United States Constitution and an original Bill of Rights in the city of Leesburg. The guns and documents were hidden in the event it may be necessary for the people to lay siege to the city of Washington and reclaim their government.

In the year 1986, a group of people searching for the hidden gun cache in Leesburg, Virginia discovered it. This group did not report their find, they enhanced it. The contents of the original site was moved and expanded. Flintlock rifles, flintlock pistols, casks of flints, casks of lead balls and kegs of powder were mixed with modern-day guns and ammunition: pistols, rifles, shotguns and the most deadly gun ever created - the Thompson submachine gun. The guns, ammunition and documents were kept hidden in the event it may be necessary for the people to lay siege to the city of Washington and reclaim their government.

The guns were hidden in the year 1814 because of an external threat of a British takeover of the United States government. The guns were hidden in the year 1986 because of an internal threat from within the United States government itself.

The threat in the year 1814 was real; British soldiers seized the city of Washington. The threat in the year 1986 was perceived; the United States government began to propose and pass laws that infringed on the liberties and freedoms of the people. The one branch of government that appeared, to this group, to be most successful in these efforts was the United States Senate.

This group of people began to become afraid of their own government. They were afraid the government may one day, infringe on the Constitutional right of the people to bare arms. To protect this Constitutional right, they hid guns and ammunition in every state.

This group of people was also afraid the government may one day make laws that mandated who lives and who dies. When that day came, the gun caches they had hidden were to be opened and used to protect themselves.

The last cache to be opened was the first cache hidden in Leesburg, Virginia. This cache was larger than the others and it was to be opened for the final push forward. This cache contained documents that were to be used in reclaiming their government in the name of the people, all of the people. These original documents were to be used to return the United States government to the ideals and values as set forth in the year 1776.

This group of people who hid guns, ammunition and documents in the year 1986 was also named the Sons of Liberty.

The Harvesting of Joseph Victorio

War is only fought in desperation
War is only fought for survival

Edward Ronny Arnold

Computer Classics ®
Nashville, Tennessee

The Harvesting of Joseph Victorio

Chapters

INTRODUCTION

Definition

har·vest (härvst)
noun.
1. To take or kill.

har·vest·ed
verb.
1.
a. To take or kill (example: extinct fowl, hare or deer) for food, sport, or population control.
b. To extract from a living body, for transplantation: kidneys, heart, pancreas, liver or eyes.
2. A person, male or female, in the United States who has attained the legal age of sixty-five and has been harvested for their usable organs. United States politicians are exempt from being harvested.

har·vest·ers
noun.
1. Executive Branch of the United States government. This branch was enacted by the United States Senate in the year 2032, to harvest U.S. population members who attain the legal age of harvesting – sixty-five years.
2. United States government employees - controllers of aged population.
3. To harvest (kill) without conscious.
4. Legendary hunters of extinct species (example: fowl, hare or deer).

The Harvesting of Joseph Victorio

Hidden Weapons Cache

"What is tyranny?"

"Tyranny is when the government has one, absolute ruler," one of the soldiers answered. "The ruler uses their authority to the detriment of others."

"Is that bad?"

"Very much so," the soldier answered.

Sixteen year-old Joshua Meadows was looking at a wooden plaque. The plaque was placed on the wall above where the soldiers had dug a large hole in the brick wall.

WHEN THE GOVERNMENT FEARS THE PEOPLE, THERE IS FREEDOM. WHEN THE PEOPLE FEAR THEIR GOVERNMENT, THERE IS TYRANNY.

THOMAS JEFFERSON

"I have never met the former president," Joshua said. "What is he like?"

"Not much to tell," one of the soldiers answered. "He wrote the Declaration of Independence. That is what we are fighting for."

Robert and Adrian slowly bricked the entrance to the secret room. It was dug in the root cellar in the west area of Mr. Jenkins' home. Soldiers had worked for several weeks in secret to prepare the room. The home was located twelve miles to the north east of the courthouse in Leesburg, Virginia.

"Hurry and finish it," Joshua said. He placed his rifle near the north wall and moved the plaster barrel toward the partially bricked wall.

"We have to wait for Mr. Jenkins," Lieutenant Parks said.

Joshua was impatient. "Everything is here." He looked inside the darkened room. It was dug out of the ground and extended a distance of sixty yards. The soft light from the lanterns inside revealed many wooden shelves. The wooden shelves were supported by strong pine saplings and held rifles and pistols. The dirt walls were supported with stone and large wooden beams supported the roof. Near the stone walls, kegs of powder, flints and musket balls rested. Near the kegs of ammunition were kegs of fresh water and preserved hams and bacon slabs. Flour was placed in barrels near the entrance.

The rifles and pistols had been prepared for a lengthy storage. The barrels were greased with the fat of freshly killed hogs. Their uncooked skin, with a layer of fat, covered the weapons. The barrels were plugged with freshly baked bread and strips of linen, to absorb moisture.

"Close it!" Joshua said. He was afraid. If they were discovered in the root cellar, the British would kill everyone involved: men, women and children.

"Four more items," Lieutenant Parks said. "We can not close it until Mr. Jenkins arrives."

The men waited. The sun had long set and the mortar began to harden. The men placed water on the mortar and mixed it to keep it soft. The sun was rising when Mr. Jenkins arrived; surrounded by ten armed men. Mr. Jenkins approached the partially closed entrance. In his hands he held four wooden boxes. The boxes were small, less than two feet in length and one foot in width.

Joshua looked as Mr. Jenkins opened one of the four boxes. Inside was a piece of parchment. Joshua looked carefully. The document was the Declaration of Independence. The second box contained the Constitution of the United States. The third box contained the Bill of

Rights. It was what was inside the fourth box that excited him; the flag of the United States of America.

Mr. Jenkins opened the fourth box.

"It's damaged!" Lieutenant Parks said angered.

The American flag in the fourth box was damaged. The ends were frayed and several musket balls punctured the third and fourth stripe. The white stars on the blue background were brown, scorched by fire. The flag smelled of wood smoke and gunpowder.

"It is all we could get," Mr. Jenkins said.

"We wanted a new flag!" Lieutenant Parks yelled. "This flag is damaged by war! Where did you get it?"

"It came from the Capitol," one of the military guards answered. "Travis himself took it from the pole before they fled the city."

Lieutenant Parks was angered. "What inspiration does a damaged flag give to patriots as they risk their lives and their fortunes to defend their country?"

"It is all we could get," Mr. Jenkins answered. "We had a new flag but Travis took it. He traded flags."

"And what will Colonel Travis do with this new flag?" Lieutenant Parks asked.

"He will place it on the Capitol when American patriots have recaptured the city," one of the guards answered.

Lieutenant Parks was angered. "And what of our hidden flag? What place does an American flag damaged by war have on the flag pole of the Capitol of the United States of America? What American patriot would follow a flag damaged by war?"

"It is all we could get," Mr. Jenkins said. He hung his head. Colonel Travis met him in secret and entrusted the documents to him. When the men saw the new flag, they rallied. Travis refused to give him the documents unless they traded flags. As Mr. Jenkins left the camp, the men were preparing to return to the City of Washington. The soldiers were screaming and yelling as the flag bearer marched forward. Parks was correct! What American patriot would rally behind a damaged flag that once flew over the nation's Capitol? "It's all we could get."

Lieutenant Parks was angered and impatient. There was no time to get another flag. The secret entrance had to be sealed. He pointed toward Joshua. "Place the four boxes."

Joshua squeezed through the narrow opening. The four boxes were handed to him and he crawled through the darkened space. He placed the four boxes at the end. As he returned to the opening, he carried the lanterns with him. He paused at the opening. All he could see was darkness. Rifles, pistols, ammunition, food and water were hidden. At the end, in a stone encased surrounding, the three charters of freedom and the damaged flag of the United States of America rested.

He exited the opening and it was sealed. Stone and mortar covered the secret entrance. Discarded items of a damaged spinning wheel and damaged wooden barrels were placed near the wall. Adrian threw dirt on the fresh mortar, staining it.

Their work complete, Lieutenant Parks addressed the men. "If it becomes necessary to lay siege to the City of Washington to reclaim our government, these guns we have hidden are to be used. Do not hesitate to fire upon those who will take from you and your neighbors, your liberty and your life!"

He turned to Joshua. "Find Travis!" One of the men etched on the breech of a rifle the coordinates. He handed Joshua the rifle. "Tell him what we have done and show him your rifle. If needed, can you lead him here?"

Joshua nodded. He exited the root cellar and made his way south through the woods. He was more than three miles away when he heard many musket shots. British soldiers discovered the large group of men. As they lay down their arms to surrender, the British soldiers opened fire. Joshua Meadows was unaware that he was the only patriot, left alive, who knew where the cache of guns was hidden. Joshua joined Colonel Marcus Travis as the Americans were reclaiming the City of Washington. The patriots rallied behind the new flag. Joshua was present as Colonel Travis lowered the British flag, from the flagpole atop the remains of the burned Capitol, and raised the American flag in its place. It was not necessary to return to the cellar.

"Who was Sir Winston Churchill?"
"A much needed man at a much needed time."

YOU ASK, WHAT IS OUR POLICY? I WILL SAY; "IT IS TO WAGE WAR, BY SEA, LAND AND AIR, WITH ALL OUR MIGHT AND WITH ALL THE STRENGTH THAT GOD CAN GIVE US: TO WAGE WAR AGAINST A MONSTROUS TYRANNY, NEVER SURPASSED IN THE DARK LAMENTABLE CATALOGUE OF HUMAN CRIME. THAT IS OUR POLICY." YOU ASK, WHAT IS OUR AIM? I CAN ANSWER WITH ONE WORD: VICTORY—VICTORY AT ALL COSTS, VICTORY IN SPITE OF ALL TERROR, VICTORY HOWEVER LONG AND HARD THE ROAD MAY BE; FOR WITHOUT VICTORY THERE IS NO SURVIVAL.

SIR WINSTON CHURCHILL (1874-1965)

SPEECH AS PRIME MINISTER TO THE HOUSE OF COMMONS (MAY 10, 1940)

Nine year-old Catherine Meadows was looking at a plaque. She moved towards her right to look at another plaque.

WHEN THE GOVERNMENT FEARS THE PEOPLE, THERE IS FREEDOM. WHEN THE PEOPLE FEAR THEIR GOVERNMENT, THERE IS TYRANNY.

THOMAS JEFFERSON

"What is tyranny?"

The plaques were made of metal and attached to a long series of metal shelves. The shelves held wooden crates. Her father was writing on a clipboard and he looked upward. "Tyranny is when the government has one, absolute ruler," he answered. "The ruler uses their authority to the detriment of others."

"Is that bad?" she asked.

"Very much so," her father answered. He turned the paper he was writing on and presented the blank page to Catherine. "Those quotes from Sir Winston Churchill and Thomas Jefferson have hidden meanings. Can you decipher the quote from Thomas Jefferson?"

"Of course," Catherine answered laughing. She looked at the quote and wrote several numbers on the blank page. "Each letter has a secret meaning. You must count some letters and use their number placement in the alphabet." She wrote several numbers on the blank page.

Her father laughed. "Do you know what these numbers mean?"

"Latitudes and longitudes," she answered. "Each series of numbers tells where a hidden cache of guns are located."

"Excellent!" her father said. "Can you guess this location?"

Catherine smiled. “Not without a proper map.” She paused, thinking. “It is just a guess. Twenty-five miles southeast of Carson City, Nevada.”

“Very good. Actually, twenty-seven miles,” her father said.

“Does two miles make a difference?” Catherine knew the answer but she asked anyway. She laughed and giggled.

“Yes,” her father answered. “You must use the exact coordinates. One foot can make a difference. Do you want to try another one?”

Catherine giggled. “Yes. I know exactly which one to select. My favorite!” She walked towards the right and turned beside one of the many steel shelves. She looked upwards at the metal plaque.

> IF PONIES RODE MEN AND GRASS ATE COWS, AND CATS WERE CHASED INTO HOLES BY THE MOUSE. IF SUMMER WERE SPRING AND THE OTHER WAY ROUND, THEN ALL THE WORLD WOULD BE UPSIDE DOWN.
>
> THE WORLD TURNED UPSIDE DOWN

Catherine giggled. “Grass eating cows!”

Her father smiled slightly. “Do you recall Mr. Jenkins telling you what it is and where it came from?”

“October 19, 1781,” Catherine answered proudly. “The British surrender at Yorktown. It is a song! The British band played the tune when they surrendered and they were ordered to ground guns.”

Her father laughed, “Mind like a steel trap!” He had a sad look in his eyes. “What does it mean?”

“Everything has changed,” Catherine answered. “What once was, is no more. Everything has been reversed, turned upside down. In the case of the Revolutionary War, all the power of the government shifted from a single ruler to the people."

Her father smiled slightly. "There is a code hidden in the words. Can you guess it?"

Catherine looked at the words. "39.6.33 north, 77.33.28 west. I need a proper map." She walked towards one of the shelves, opened a small wooden box and removed a map. She looked at the map. "Leesburg, Virginia. This coordinate is in the city. It is located at the corner of Liberty Street and Royal Street. It's a parking lot!"

Her father nodded his head in approval.

Catherine frowned. "A parking lot?"

Her father laughed. "Strategically placed. It is near the historic courthouse underneath Liberty Lot. That cache is ten times the size of all the others. It is the last one to be opened. It is there for the final push forward."

"Forward to where?" Catherine asked puzzled.

Her father smiled. "During the War of 1812, Leesburg, Virginia was a temporary location of the United States government and all of its archives, including the Declaration of Independence, the United States Constitution and the Bill of Rights." He smiled slightly. "Hidden in the cache are originals not copies." He pointed at the map she was holding. "Leesburg, Virginia is thirty-two miles northwest of Washington D.C."

She returned the map to the box. "How many caches are there?"

"Not sure," her father answered. He pointed towards several similar plaques in the room. "Each one of these plaques gives the location of another cache. In each of those caches, there are different plaques with different codes."

"Is this one of the locations in the other caches?" she asked curiously.

"No," her father answered. "Only one of those caches has a plaque that gives the location of this cache."

"Why?" Catherine asked.

Her father took the paper from her and he drew a series of lines. "Each cache points to the location to five additional caches. You must know how to read the plaques and use the codes to find them. If one of the caches is accidentally discovered, the other five are safe."

"Six," Catherine said. "If one of the plaques reveals the location of this cache, and there are five more, that is six." She smiled. "Each cache, including itself, makes six."

"Correct," her father said. "This cache, is one, and points to the location of five others. Five plus one makes six."

"How many guns?" Catherine asked. She looked at the long row of metal shelves and the wooden crates.

"Not sure," her father answered. "There are more than three thousand in this cache. Each cache is different."

"Why?" Catherine asked. She placed her hand on one of the wooden crates. There was lettering on the end of one of the large crates.

144 THOMPSON SUBMACHINE GUNS / DRUM MAGAZINE.

"Many reasons," her father answered. He was interested in her questions but he seemed detached, sad. There was something wrong with her father. Catherine could sense it. She could tell it in his voice.

He leaned downwards towards her. "Guns are of no use if there is no ammunition. Some caches have guns and some have ammunition." He pointed towards one of the many sections. "There is enough ammunition here for a few small battles. In order to be successful, all of the caches must be combined."

Catherine looked at the many metal shelves. Several were separated from the main area. She knew this section contained bullets, gunpowder and equipment to repair and make guns.

Her father leaned closer to her and he hugged her. He moved backwards, with tears in his eyes. "One day, the government will decide who lives and who dies. When that day comes, these guns we have hidden will save your life and the life of your friends. Use them without regret. Use them without remorse."

He wiped his eyes with his shirt sleeve and took her hand. They walked along the many metal shelves and she looked at the many crates. Each crate had words printed on the end. 144 Thompson Submachine Guns / drum magazine, most of the wording on the larger crates read. She paused to look at a smaller crate.

.357 STAINLESS STEEL MAGNUM / 240 EACH W/ HOLSTER W/ GUN BELT W/ 2000 ROUNDS - STEEL JACKETED.

Catherine smiled. She pointed at the small crate. "Two thousand rounds divided by two hundred forty pistols gives eight rounds. That is not much ammunition."

Her father laughed. He pointed towards several large crates resting beside the one she was pointing at.

10000 STEEL JACKETED .357

"Forty nine rounds from those two hundred forty guns, is a hell of a lot of fire power!"

She pointed towards several additional crates. "If you run out, there's more!"

Her father laughed as he opened a small package he had been carrying; inside the package was another plaque. He walked towards the right. On the steel shelving was a placement marker. He placed the plaque on the marker and mounted it with several bolts.

Catherine walked to the plaque.

LET OUR ADV ANCE WO RRYING BEC OME ADVAN CE THINK ING AND PLAN NIN G.

WI NSTON CHURCHIL L

"This also has a hidden message. Can you decipher it?"

Catherine smiled. She looked at the sentence. As she looked at the sentence, she appeared puzzled and frowned. "You made a mistake! The hidden message is not a map coordinate."

"Are you sure?"

Catherine looked at the sentence again. She took the paper and a pencil from her father. Catherine sat on the cement floor and wrote on the paper. "Someone made an error. The hidden message is not a map coordinate."

Her father smiled. "Each cache has that exact same plaque in the exact same location. It points to another cache."

"No it doesn't."

"Are you sure?" her father asked.

Catherine looked upwards, calculating distance and map direction. She looked towards her right. "Absolutely," she answered. "Someone made an error. It makes no sense."

Her father laughed. "Perhaps you are the one who made the error. Remember that each letter has a numeric placement in the alphabet." He pointed towards the quote. "You must use one of the codes. Did you notice there are additional spaces? The extra spaces in the quote appear as errors but they are not errors. What is the hidden message?"

"I know that!" Catherine answered angered. "I noticed the additional spaces and used their numeric alphabetic placement. There is nothing there! Someone made an error!"

"What is the hidden message?" Her father's voice was calm. He was not angry.

"It is not a map coordinate," Catherine answered. "It is not a map direction." She turned the page towards her father. "It is an instruction."

WEST THIRTEEN YARDS – PUSH.

Fear, Desperation, Hope

She looked west, her right. Thirteen yards from where she was sitting, where the quote from Winston Churchill was mounted, was a cement wall. "There is nothing there!"

"Are you sure? Follow the instructions."

Catherine placed the paper and pencil on the cement floor and walked thirteen yards west. She was standing in front of the cement wall. She began to push, but nothing happened. She turned towards her father with an angry look on her face. "I told you someone made an error!"

"My error," her father said. He walked to stand beside her and he faced the wall. "This was not designed for a nine year-old girl." He leaned towards the wall and pushed. The section of the wall he pushed on moved slightly inward and slightly outward to reveal an opening.

Catherine looked inside to see darkness.

Her father walked to where the last plaque was mounted and he picked up a flashlight. He walked to the opening, turned it on, and pointed the beam inwards. Catherine looked inside and gasped!

The hidden room within the hidden room was larger than the one they were standing in. This room was different! There were no metal shelves and wooden crates. This room was filled with metal boxes. Some boxes were larger than others and some boxes were very small. To the left of the opening, the wall was lined with large metal boxes.

Her father handed her the flashlight and she entered the room. She walked to one of the large metal boxes that lined the wall of the room and pointed the flashlight beam towards lettering on the front of one of the boxes.

PENICILLIN V POTASSIUM TABLETS
100000 500 MG (800,000) UNITS
WARNING: DO NOT OPEN CONTAINER!
EXPIRATION DATE: AUGUST 19, 2079

She pointed the flashlight beam towards another large metal box.

144 MEDICAL CONDITION DIAGNOSIS KITS
WARNING: DO NOT USE UNLESS PROPERLY TRAINED

Catherine pointed the flashlight beam towards another large metal box.

1200 EMERGENCY FIELD SURGICAL KITS
STOMACH WOUND
WARNING: ONLY TO BE USED BY CLASS V TRAINED TEAMS

The room was massive and the many metal boxes gave her a feeling of foreboding. Danger. Desperation. Catherine's hand holding the flashlight shook and she began to perspire. She walked quickly from the room. "Please. Close it!"

Her father pushed on a section of the opened cement wall and the hidden door closed. There was nothing to be seen but a cement wall.

"What is in there?" Catherine asked slowly. She was visibly shaken as she sat down and leaned against the cement wall. The guns had been fun, this room was not fun. This room held something her father and his friends had held from her – pain, suffering and death. War was not about winning. War was also about losing. War was losing the people you love, war was losing your friends and war was losing the people you are fighting for.

War was only fought in desperation; war was only fought for survival.

Her father's expression was sad. He leaned downward towards her. "We have learned a lot about war. We know about weapons and how to fight the enemy but there is one lesson we have not learned. In every war, the same mistake was made. This mistake was made by Julius Caesar, Napoleon, the French and English armies and George Washington. Winston Churchill, himself, almost made the same mistake."

He paused and stood. "Guns and bullets are of no use if the people fighting have no food, water and medicine."

Catherine's eyes widened.

Her father smiled slightly and turned. He pointed towards the many shelves. "In the beginning of a war, spirits are high. The soldier is fighting for a cause they believe in. The soldier is willing to die for his or her family, friends and strangers."

He turned towards her. "If the soldier does not have food, water and medicine, their spirits begin to weaken. They will begin to take food from wherever they can find it. When this happens, the liberators are seen as conquerors and the cause looses support from the people. This happened to both the Colonists and British during the Revolutionary War and both sides of the American Civil War. Each hidden cache has within it, another hidden cache. Hopefully, we have learned one lesson of war. This cache contains food, water and medicine. There is more than enough food, water and medicine for the soldier." He pointed towards the hidden door. "There is additional food, water and medicine to help the people they are fighting for. Guns alone do not win wars. You need the people, all of the people!"

Catherine looked at the hidden door. Her feelings of foreboding fear and desperation from the room slowly dissolved. She understood what her father and his friends had done. What her father and his friends had hidden inside the hidden rooms was not fear and desperation; what her father and his friends had hidden inside the hidden rooms were nothing more than daily necessities. In times of war – daily necessities brought regularity and stability, to an irregular, unstable life. In any conflict stability is a key to success. What was hidden was hope. In times of war, hope was the difference in liberty and tyranny. In times of war, hope was the difference in life and death.

Catherine smiled. "Let our advance worrying become advance thinking and planning."

"Exactly," her father laughed as he took the flashlight from her. He turned and began to remove the kerosene lanterns from their holders.

"Why are you taking the lights?" Catherine asked puzzled as she stood.

"This is the last time we will come here," her father answered.

She looked at the large room. It was buried underground with only one entrance. The sides, floor and roof were made of cement. The entrance was reached by a series of small ladders. There were three levels. At one time, there was a very large entrance. Catherine remembered the main entrance being large enough for one of the big trucks. Over a period of weeks, her father and several of his friends slowly closed the main entrance. There was enough room to bring one of the crates up and out of the large room.

He placed the lanterns and flashlights in a wooden crate and moved the crate towards the ladder. As he lowered the wicks on the kerosene lamps, the room slowly darkened. He pointed a flashlight beam towards the end of the room. There was nothing to be seen but metal shelves and crates.

"Wait!" Catherine yelled. She took a flashlight from the crate, turned it on, and ran to where she had placed the sheet of paper and pencil on the floor. She picked them up. "Let our advance worrying become advance thinking and planning."

Her father laughed as Catherine returned to stand beside him. She pointed the flashlight beam outward and upwards.

Satisfied that everything was safe, they placed the flashlights in the crate. He helped Catherine to climb the metal ladder. He followed her and closed the heavy metal door. It made a loud clang sound when he closed it.

"Are you going to lock it?" Catherine asked puzzled.

"No," her father answered. "Someone may need access very quickly. A locked door could mean the difference in their life and their death."

She nodded her head as she walked to the truck, opened the door, and sat inside. She watched her father mount the small earth mover. The engine made a deep growling sound when he started the engine and the tall pipe, above the engine, blew a dark, black smoke into the air. The metal treads began to move as her father placed large amounts of dirt over the metal door.

When he was finished, the area looked flat. There was no indication of a door or a secret room. Her father had many secrets. The codes he taught her were one of many. Catherine had a very good memory. She had deciphered the codes on the various plaques. She knew exactly where the cache was in Carson City. She knew something else, less than three hundred yards from the secret entrance, her father had just covered, was cache number 842. The cache they had just buried was cache number 841. She figured out the code. The cache that had an odd number mainly held guns. The cache with an even number was mainly ammunition. She did not tell her father what she had figured out. Each city held two caches; one for guns and one for ammunition. Now she knew that each cache, held another cache. Each cache was approximately thirty miles from each other. She knew, a plaque on the inside of the cache in Carson City pointed to another cache three hundred yards away. Her father was correct. *What good is a gun if you don't have bullets? What good is a soldier if they have no food, water and medicine?*

She watched her father move the small earth mover to the back of the ramp and load it. The truck made a jerk when the weight was evened. He locked the machine with chains and entered the driver's side. "Do you know how to find it?'

Catherine giggled. She leaned towards her father and whispered in his ear. He laughed slightly. "I hope you never need to come here again."

He started the truck engine and he drove the large truck and trailer slowly from the empty field. She turned backwards and looked at the flat ground, with the tall statue towards the center. The statue was of Thomas Jefferson and the field was a section of the park that her father and his friends were renovating. Patriot's Park it was named, located in downtown Boston, Massachusetts. The hidden door was exactly thirteen yards from the statue and thirteen feet deep. She had figured out the codes! Everything was based on the number thirteen. Thirteen original colonies; made sense to her!

The Harvesters

The room was filled with young men and women. They sat in chairs speaking to each other when their commander entered the room. The people in the room immediately became quiet.

The commander walked towards the front of the room. He smiled slightly as he looked at the young men and women. "We have received reports of harvesters quitting their jobs. If you have any problems, do not hesitate to contact me."

One of the harvesters raised their hand. "Quit. Why would someone quit? It was my understanding, we could not quit."

"Quit," the commander said. "It is against the Harvesting Act of 2032 for a harvester to quit or organize into some type of union." He seemed irritated by the question. "We have received reports of harvesters delivering the organs and then quitting."

"How did they quit?" one of the harvesters asked.

"Just quit," the commander answered. "They were sent to harvest a person. We know they harvested them because the organs were returned. However, the harvesters were never seen or heard from again."

"Strange," one of the harvesters said. "When did this happen?"

"It began three years ago," the commander answered. "Six harvesters were sent to harvest Mrs. Joseph Victorio. They returned the parts but were never seen or heard from again." He paused slightly. "In the last year we have received many reports of harvesters quitting. The reports are mainly from the southeast but yesterday, we received three reports from the Midwest."

"Why would they quit?" one of the harvesters asked.

"I have no idea," the commander answered. "We have received reports that some of these people have resisted."

"Resisted?" one of the harvesters asked surprised. "Why would someone resist harvesting? It's the law."

"Use your stunner," one of the harvesters said. "If we sense any type of resistance, I immediately use the stunner." He held upward a tube-type device. He squeezed the handle and a small electric bolt leapt from the end.

The commander laughed. "Excellent suggestion! In the event of resistance, use the stunner."

One of the harvesters raised her hand. "The use of the stunner is forbidden under Section 203 of the Harvesting Act of 2032."

"Why?" one of the harvesters asked. "I have never been told that."

"The electrical charge can destroy one or more of the vital organs," the woman answered. "If we use stunners, we are breaking the law."

"We are the law!" the commander said. "Each one of you is a designated agent of the United States Senate. Your number one goal is to harvest the person and or persons you have been assigned to. The goal is to harvest, how it is done is your discretion."

"How much discretion?" one of the harvesters asked.

"Stun them! Choke them! Smother them with bed coverings!" the commander yelled. "I don't care how you do it! These people are old and useless! It is our job to harvest them for population control."

"Because of these reports of resistance, we have requested that anyone scheduled for harvesting be denied any type of medical treatment. That includes prescribed medication."

"You have your assignments!" he yelled. "I want to see organs delivered."

The men and women stood as the commander walked out of the room.

One of the women looked to a man standing to her right. "My team has a full schedule this week. We have nineteen. How many do you have?"

"Light schedule this week," the man answered. "We only have twelve." He looked at his communicator and paused. "This is interesting. Number eight on our list. Mr. Joseph Victorio. 497 Elysian Fields Road."

The woman looked puzzled. "Joseph Victorio. Do you think this is the same person whose wife was harvested three years ago? Do you think he knows anything about the harvesters who quit?"

"No," the man answered. "I do not think it is the same person. If it is the same person, his wife was harvested three years ago. According to what the commander said, she was harvested and her organs returned. It has been three years. He would not know anything about it."

They began to walk out of the room when the woman stopped. "Did you know Jerry and Sam? They were on the red team."

"No," the man answered.

The woman leaned towards the man and spoke quietly. "I remember being asked about them three years ago. They were one of the first teams that quit."

"How did they quit?" the man whispered.

"Just quit," the woman answered. "They harvested a woman and returned her organs, disposed of the remains and quit."

"How did you know that?" the man asked.

"I was asked if I had seen them," the woman answered. She shrugged her shoulders. "Their van was found in the clinic lot. Inside the van were the organs. They were never seen again."

"Hum," the man muttered. "That sounds strange."

"Real strange," the woman said. She leaned toward the man and whispered in his ear. "The organs in the van were male not female."

Advance Notice

SECRETARIATE OF SENATE

FIRST SECTION – GENERAL AFFAIRS

JOSEPH VICTORIO
497 ELYSIAN FIELDS ROAD
NASHVILLE, TN 37211

SIR OR MADAM,

MAY 4, 2042 YOU WILL HAVE OBTAINED THE LEGAL AGE OF SIXTY-FIVE. SECTIONS 501 AND 505 OF THE HARVESTING ACT OF 2032, REQUIRES YOU TO BE HARVESTED ON THAT DATE. DISPOSE OF ALL PERSONAL ITEMS PRIOR TO **MAY 4, 2042.** YOUR ORGANS WILL BE HARVESTED AND YOUR REMAINS CREMATED. PLEASE MAKE ARRANGEMENTS FOR A DESIGNATED PERSON OR PERSONS TO RECEIVE YOUR REMAINS.

YOUR CO-OPERATION IN THIS MATTER WILL BE GREATLY APPRECIATED.

U.S. DEPARTMENT OF HARVESTING
3336 MASSACHUSETTS AVE., N. W.
WASHINGTON, D.C. 20006-3686

Joseph was angered as he read the letter. He removed a writing pen from his desk and he wrote on the letter.

LIKE HELL YOU WILL!

"Don't let it get to you," the woman standing behind him said. "You know what to do." She hugged him very hard and turned to walk out of the room. As she walked, her left leg appeared to drag. The woman walked with a limp.

"I will contact the others and inform them. They will help us to remove everything from our home and prepare."

Joseph moved from the desk to his work bench. He nodded his head as he began to turn the drill bit. "Please hold this?"

She walked to the work bench and held the metal bar as Joseph slowly turned the handle. The metal bar was attached to a clamp. A device held the drill bit stationary as he slowly turned it clockwise. As he turned the drill bit, the hole in the end of the metal bar deepened.

"How many do you have ready?"

"Six," Joseph answered. He frowned as he looked at a small box near his work bench. The box was filled with metal bars of different lengths and widths. "There are only two pieces I can use."

"What is wrong with the other pieces?"

"Most of the bars are made of aluminum," Joseph answered. "The other pieces are not the correct width. I tried one of them but the bullet cracked the barrel." He completed several turns of the drill and the end of the bar slowly opened. Joseph took the bar from the clamp and placed it in a tap. He turned it several times, making a screw end.

Joseph removed the bar and cut the end with a metal saw. The total length was four inches. He attached the end to the cylinder and rotated the cylinder. Clicking noises could be heard. "Seven."

"Looks good!"

"Looks are not everything," Joseph said in a disgusted tone. "They can only be used a maximum of eight times."

"Hammond has used his ten times."

Joseph leaned backwards in his chair. "I told him not to use it more than eight times. The bullets being fired places too much strain on the barrel and the cylinder. It will jam."

The woman placed her arms around Joseph. "It's all we have."

Joseph frowned. "What I would give for gunpowder and metal."

"Can you use the aluminum?"

"Yes," Joseph answered slowly. He held to her arms and gently squeezed. "I can heat the metal and form it into bullets. The aluminum bullets are lighter than lead but they shatter on impact. They make one heck of a hole."

She pointed to a box that contained stunners. "Why can't we use those?"

"The battery must be recharged after a period of time," Joseph answered. "We do not have a charger. They are useless."

She looked at a small box and removed one bullet. "It feels sticky. What's wrong with it?"

"The primer is defective," Joseph answered. He took the bullet from her. "The gunpowder does not burn quickly enough to fire the charge. Mary and Alice are doing the best they can but we can not produce enough gunpowder." He paused. "Mary suggested coating the bullet with paraffin. It helps to keep the powder dry." He threw the bullet into the box. "What good is a gun without bullets?"

"Have there been any reported misfires?"

"Two," Joseph answered. "But we can not have one misfire. I added three more cartridge cells to the cylinder. That gives us three extra."

"Rest, you need rest."

"No time," Joseph said. "There are too many people we have to protect." He looked at the seven home-made guns. "They are all we have and we are all they have."

"Let's pray?"

Joseph stood from his chair and they kneeled.

"Oh God," Joseph prayed. "In our hour of need we ask for your blessing? In our hour of need we ask for your protection? Please help us to help others in their hour of need. I humbly beseech you to help us to obtain gunpowder and metal. We have the skills and the willingness. We do not have the raw materials. Without gunpowder and metal we are useless to save others."

"Oh God," she prayed. "We humbly ask your forgiveness for what we have done and what we will do. We know it is against your law to kill. We must take a life to save a life. Look down upon these others and change their hearts. Bring to them peace so they will not take innocent lives. We will accept your punishment for what we have done. We humbly ask that you look upon those we protect and keep them safe."

"Amen," they both said.

Joseph Victorio

"Come in," a man's voice said. "I have been waiting for you!"

The door opened slowly as the six harvesters entered the unit of Joseph Victorio. Mr. Victorio was sitting in a chair towards the far end of the main room. Six chairs had been placed in front of where he sat.

The six harvesters entered the room and walked to sit in the six chairs.

Mr. Victorio smiled. He was sixty-five years old and appeared young for his age. There were slight traces of white in his dark brown hair. His face was cleanly shaven and his hair was cut short.

He appeared tall, perhaps five feet eleven inches in height. His body shape was thin. Mr. Victorio looked like anyone you may see walking on the street. The only thing unusual about him was his clothing. His clothing was old, but clean. He was wearing pants that were dark blue in color. They were made of denim. His shirt was white, a dress-type shirt. On his collar was a tie. The tie was older and faded in areas. It was stained from food and the design was of an American eagle. The eagle appeared to be in flight with its talons stretched forward and outward.

He was wearing a coat that was of a light brown color. The coat was old and made, also, of a type of denim, corduroy. Mr. Victorio was wearing, on his feet, leather boots. The boots were a dark brown and in poor condition.

One of the six harvesters laughed. "Is that the best you have?"

Joseph smiled. "My work clothes. I always wear them when I work."

"What work do you do?" one of the six harvesters asked giggling. "You do not work anymore."

"A part-time job," Joseph answered. "To keep me from being bored, I have taken on part-time work."

"What kind of part-time work?" one of the six harvesters asked.

"Exterminator," Joseph answered.

"What work did you do before you became a part-time exterminator?" one of the six harvesters asked.

"Machinist," Joseph answered. "I made things from metal. I made tools and tools to be used to make tools." He smiled at one of the harvesters. In the harvesters hand was a communicator. "I helped to design the shell casing for your communicator."

He paused and smiled. "Which one of you is carrying a stunner?"

"I am," one of the six harvesters answered. He removed the stunner from his pocket and he held it upwards. "Why?"

"I designed the casing for it," Joseph answered. "I also helped to design the main chip. If we had known what we were designing the chip for, we would have added a back door."

The harvester looked at the stunner. He smiled slightly. "Good work."

"Too good."

The unit of Joseph Victorio was barren. Decorations had been removed from the walls and the only furniture seen was the seven chairs. The walls held discolored sections that were square, rectangular and round. These discolored sections were photographs removed. The photographs, placed for an extended period of time, created the discoloration. The sections were of a lighter color than the walls and ceiling. The unit of Joseph Victorio was the color of a pastel yellow.

The floor was barren. At one time, a large covering covered the floor. This was seen by another discoloration on the floor. On the floor, under the six chairs, was a large clear plasticized cloth. The cloth covered the floor.

The six chairs the six harvesters were sitting on, also, was covered with a clear plasticized cloth. The chairs were made of metal and the plasticized cloth covered the chairs.

The chair Mr. Victorio was sitting in was made of wood and very ornate. The chair had arms that extended outward and formed a type of animal's claw. The four legs were also made of wood, extended downward, ending in a type of animal's claw.

A cloth cover decorated the wooden back of the chair. The back of the chair extended upward, above the sitting position of Mr. Victorio and ended with a curl. The curl appeared to be carved wood. The cloth was a once bright mixture of the colors of red, yellow, blue and green. The design was faded but easily seen, a wooded scene with many extinct animals – fowl and deer.

Mr. Victorio seemed calm; relaxed. He smiled slightly.

The six harvesters were relaxed, calm. They began to notice a smell. "What is that smell?" one asked.

Joseph smiled. "Moth balls and vinegar."

"Why?" one of the harvesters asked.

"The moth balls are to protect my clothing from insects," Joseph answered. "I use vinegar on my legs. I have shingles."

"Does it work?" one of the harvesters asked. "Does vinegar cure shingles?"

"No," Joseph answered. "It does not cure shingles but it makes the skin feel better."

"You should have went to the clinic," one of the harvesters said. "Did you report it?"

"I did," Joseph answered. "I was denied treatment based on my age. If I had been younger, under the age of thirty, the government agent would have approved treatment."

Life

"All life is very precious."

"You are dead a lot longer than you are alive," one of the harvesters said.

Joseph narrowed his eyes. "Life is a gift from God!"

"Death is a gift from the government," one of the harvesters said.

"Life is a gift. Death is a consequence of living."

"Death is a gift," one of the harvesters said. "Tomorrow morning, you will not have to get up. You will have no pain or suffering. Death is a gift."

"Perhaps," Joseph said. "Perhaps tomorrow it is you who will not have to get up. Life is a gift; death is a consequence of living. Death can be a consequence of a person's actions."

"Accidents are unavoidable," one of the harvesters said. "Illness is unavoidable. Old age is unavoidable. Death is a gift. Death is unavoidable."

Joseph smiled. "Death may be unavoidable but it is not a gift; death is a transition."

"Transition to what?" one of the six harvesters asked. "When you die, there is nothing."

"Depends on your view," Joseph said. "Philosophers Plato and Aristotle theorized we each hold within us, physical traits from our parents. They also theorized we each hold memories and consciousness from our parents and distant relatives."

"What does that mean?" one of the six harvesters asked puzzled.

"If you agree with their theories," Joseph answered, "it means my life is not of one but many. Within my body, I hold memories of my parents and distant relatives. When I die, many will die with me. Only by living, can we continue."

"Tell that to the people in the cemeteries," one of the harvesters said. "What good are memories if you can not pass them on to another person?"

"I already have," Joseph said. "I have two daughters."

"You can not have children," one of the six harvesters said. "You are too old. How can you pass memories to your two daughters?"

"By living," Joseph answered. "I can pass to them my current memories. In turn, they will pass them to their children and their children's children."

"Mr. Victorio," one of the six harvesters said irritated. "If you are talking about genetics, it has never been proven that memories are passed in the DNA of the parent to the offspring. Physical traits have been proven, without doubt, science has yet to prove genetic consciousness."

"I am not talking about genetics," Joseph said. "I am talking about memories, feelings." He paused. "Knowledge."

"Dead people have no knowledge," one of the six harvesters said. "They are dead."

"Yes," Joseph said. "They are dead but before they died, they passed their knowledge to others."

One of the six harvesters looked puzzled. "Knowledge diminishes with age. Science has proven that a person looses knowledge when they obtain the age of sixty-five years. There is nothing to pass because there is nothing to give."

"That theory has been disproved many times," Joseph said. "Knowledge comes in many forms."

One of the six harvesters laughed. "Are you saying an old person's reminisces of days long past is knowledge?"

"Exactly!"

New Knowledge

"And what knowledge do you propose to pass?" one of the harvesters asked.

"Nothing new, in fact, something very old," Joseph answered.

"And when did you learn this old knowledge that is new?" one of the harvesters asked, amused.

"Four years ago," Joseph answered.

"Mr. Victorio, you have just proven our point," one of the harvesters said. "You were sixty-one years old four years ago. You have nothing to give at the age of sixty-five. What you claim is knowledge, has no value today."

Joseph stood. "Much, much value. More today than four years ago. More value tomorrow, next week, next year than today."

"What is this value?" one of the harvesters asked.

"A key!"

"A key to what?" one of the harvesters asked amused. "A key to a lock box with some hidden secret from your past?"

"No. A key to survival," Joseph answered. "I rediscovered a key to survival. Without this key, there is no survival."

"Does the government know about this key?" one of the harvesters asked.

Joseph laughed. "I hope not. The key is not for the survival of the government, it is a key for the survival of the people."

"The people and the government are the same," one of the harvesters said. "It does not matter. You are sixty-five years of age. What you did or think you did four years ago has no value today. There is nothing you can do."

"Improve the key," Joseph said. "I have made changes. Each change makes the key better, more efficient."

"Mr. Victorio, what are you saying?" one of the harvesters asked puzzled.

"Time! I want time," Joseph answered. "I am asking you for time."

"Time is something we can not give," one of the harvesters said. "You know why we are here."

Joseph sat in his chair. "Yes," he said slowly. "I know why you are here."

"Then why did you ask for time?" one of the harvesters asked.

"I wanted to give you an opportunity," Joseph answered. "I wanted to know where you are."

"Mr. Victorio, we are here," one of the six harvesters said. He looked at the other five. "We are here."

Joseph smiled slightly. "Does it not bother you why you are here?"

"No," all six harvesters answered.

Joseph looked puzzled at the six people sitting in front of him. They displayed no emotion in their faces. His statements of life meant nothing to them. They only knew death, not life.

Love

Joseph laughed. It was not a slight laugh but a loud and long laugh. The harvesters looked at him strangely. His face was at first bright, then saddened. He laughed with smiles, and then he laughed with tears. The expression on his face changed from happiness to one of sadness. He slowly stopped laughing and wiped the tears from his cheeks with the sleeve of his coat.

"What's funny?" one of the harvesters asked.

Joseph raised his head. "That," he answered. He pointed toward the leg brace one of the female harvesters wore on her left leg.

The female harvester looked at her left leg. "I don't see anything funny!"

"What happened?" Joseph asked. His question was unexpected and completely out of line.

The woman frowned. "A woman who was to be harvested changed her mind before we gave her the medication and she kicked me. What does this have to do with anything?"

"That's how I met my wife," Joseph answered. "I had a leg brace and she was refused the treatment." He paused. "I gave her mine!"

"That is against government law!" one of the harvesters yelled. He had lost his cool. *This man is delaying us.* He calmed himself down. "What is funny?"

"She lived a full and happy life," Joseph answered. "I met her at the clinic. I had injured my leg playing sports. Since I was young, a leg brace and treatment was approved. She was older and female. She injured her leg but because…she was female … the brace and therapy were denied."

"Age and circumstances," one of the harvesters remarked. "It happens all the time. How old was she?"

Joseph looked saddened. "She was three years older than I was. I was seventeen and she was twenty."

The eyes of the female harvester wearing the leg brace widened. "She lived for forty-five years?"

Joseph smiled slightly. "My leg brace was too large for her damaged leg and her leg did not heal fully, but she, we, was able to take long walks. If I had not done what I did, Audrey would have been a cripple." He paused smiling. "That is how I met her. We fell in love with each other!"

One of the harvesters stood. "You broke the law!"

"Imprison me!" Joseph said laughing. "There is nothing wrong with helping someone less fortunate than you."

The harvester was angered. "If you were not scheduled for harvesting, I would arrest you!"

Joseph shrugged his shoulders. "She never told and I never told. I expected her to say something three years ago when she was harvested, but she remained silent." He lowered his head. "I guess I owe her that."

"Implicating her in a major crime doesn't sound like love," one of the harvesters said, with a smirk on his face.

"Being honest about a person's relationship is love," Joseph said. He raised his head. *Have any of these people ever loved anyone?* "I am not ashamed of what I did. I'm proud! We lived in fear most of our lives but it feels good to tell the truth. I'm proud of what I did, not ashamed. It doesn't matter to Audrey; she was harvested three years ago."

"You never told anyone?" the female harvester wearing the leg brace asked.

"No one," Joseph answered.

"Why did you not tell anyone?" she asked. Her question and the sound of her voice seemed uncertain. *His voice is calm, too calm. He is planning something. Perhaps, he thinks he can run.*

She slowly moved her injured leg to the side, placing her right leg over it, as to somehow protect it.

Joseph shrugged his shoulders. "Public scandal. You can't help anyone anymore. I would have lost my job and any future health benefits. She would have done worse, prison. It is against the law to violate the public health decisions. While I was the guilty one, she would have been seen as more guilty. It seemed the prudent thing to do."

"Are you ready?" one of the harvesters asked. The expression on his face was bland. The questions sounded like one he had asked hundreds perhaps thousands of times.

Joseph leaned backwards in his chair. "Not yet. I am curious as to how many people you have murdered … harvested today."

"It is not murder to harvest a person and it is sanctioned by Federal law," one of the harvesters said angered. *What's his problem? He is old and useless.*

"Three," the woman wearing the leg brace answered. "We have harvested three people today; two men and one woman. You are the fourth."

"What is it like?" Joseph asked. "What is it like to harvest a person; a living, breathing human being?"

"Nothing," one of the harvesters answered. "I feel nothing. It is a job." He shrugged his shoulders.

"I feel nothing also," one of the harvesters said. "The healthcare laws are explicit. When a person reaches the legal age of sixty-five, they are to be harvested. Population control! The older people are harvested and the young ones take over. Harvesting keeps a steady work force and improves productivity. Without it, the United States would be a nation of older people who have no value."

Joseph nodded his head. "I understand the law. I didn't vote for it but there was nothing to vote for. It was enacted in secret."

One of the harvesters laughed loudly. "That is a rumor started sometime in the late 2030s. Everyone knew what was going on."

Joseph smiled slightly. "That rumor was not a rumor."

"Mr. Victorio, this has nothing to do with anything," the harvester added. "The law is the law. You have reached the legal age of sixty-five. In essence, you have outlived any usefulness to society. You are a burden and if you remained employed, it prevents a younger person from working. If you are not harvested it places a strain on the healthcare system."

"You didn't answer my questions," Joseph said irritated. "What is it like? What do you do?"

"Sedate you," the female harvester wearing the leg brace answered. "It takes ten minutes. When you are unconscious, we remove any organ that can be transplanted. The process is painless. You go to sleep and never wake up."

"Are you sure?" Joseph asked slowly. "How do you know it's painless? Perhaps the person is still conscious and they can feel pain."

"No pain!" one of the harvesters said forcibly. "The medication is very powerful. We can't kill you because the organs must remain as close to a hospital transplant extraction as possible."

Joseph's eyes narrowed. "When my wife was harvested, the procedures were done at a government health clinic. You sound like you intend to do it here. Are you?"

One of the harvesters smiled slightly. "Yes. An analysis was completed last year on the cost of harvesting at the clinic or the person's home. It is more cost effective to be done here." He nodded slightly. *Why does he care?* "The study shows that the person feels more comfortable at home."

Joseph laughed. "How can a person complete the study if they are dead?"

"Obvious," one of the harvesters said, visibly perturbed. "They were asked before the procedure, not after." *What is this guy's problem?*

"Where is she?" Joseph asked angered. "Where is Audrey?"

"I do not understand your question," one of the harvesters answered. "If you are referring to your wife, she was harvested three years ago. Obviously, she is not here."

"I know that," Joseph said angered. "I am not a fool! Where is she? What did you do with her remains?"

The harvester, who was standing, sat in the chair. "Her remains were returned to you. You Mr. Victorio can answer your own question."

"She was not returned to me," Joseph said slowly. "I made many inquiries but no one knew the answer. I thought one of you would know where her remains are."

"All remains are returned to the next of biological kin. You should have them," the harvester who wore the leg brace said.

"No," Joseph said. "I do not have them. Where are they?"

"Mr. Victorio, I have no idea. All we do is the procedure," the harvester who wore the leg brace answered. "It is my understanding the remains are cremated and returned to the next of biological kin or a designated recipient for proper burial."

"Can you verify that?" Joseph asked. He pointed toward a communicator one of the harvesters was holding.

One of the harvesters stood. He walked toward the door and slowly turned. "If you did not receive her cremated remains, it is possible her remains were placed in a common grave. It is more cost effective to bury many in one grave than to use individual graves. After you have been harvested, the same will happen to you." He shrugged his shoulders.

"Since the city only has one common grave, your ashes will mix with hers."

"And a thousand others," Joseph remarked.

"Does it make any difference?" the harvester asked. "If you have been harvested, why should it matter?"

"It doesn't matter to me at all," Joseph answered. "I have two daughters and they have the impression my remains will be returned to them. It doesn't matter to me but I think it will matter to them." He paused. "I was concerned and worried about Audrey's remains. What happened to her remains, it mattered to me. I wanted to hold a funeral. Funerals are for the living not the dead." He paused. "I wanted to honor Audrey. I wanted our friends to gather together and talk about her life and what she had meant to them. I wanted to talk about what she meant…to me!"

"Funeral expenses are a waste of money," one of the harvesters said bored. *What an idiot! He must have an IQ of minus ten.*

"Dignity," Joseph said sadly. "A funeral is to display dignity and honor to the deceased."

"There is no dignity or honor among the living," one of the harvesters said. "The people of the United States have no dignity or honor. They hold their hands outward waiting for the government to care for them. They take to their grave what they carried in their life, nothing."

Joseph narrowed his eyes. "The people of the United States have dignity and honor in themselves. The government has made them afraid to display it. You are correct in that all they take with them to their grave is nothing. Nothing is what is left after the government took everything from them."

Two of the harvesters frowned; one of the two motioned for the others to stand. They all stood. "Excuse us for a few minutes." He motioned for the others to follow him. He walked to the door and went outside, the others followed.

"He is delaying us," one of the harvesters said. "Sedate him and harvest him! I am tired of these questions."

"Let me use the stunner?" one of the harvesters asked as he removed a small, light-type object from his coat. "Stun him and harvest him."

"Get it over with," one of the harvesters said.

"He is nervous," the harvester who wore the leg brace said. She looked at her left leg. She received a fracture when the woman kicked her. "Many of the people we have recently harvested seemed reluctant. He wants to talk and I think we should let him talk."

"Then what?" the harvester holding the stunner asked. He squeezed the device and a small bolt of electrical fire leapt from the end.

"Take him!" the harvester who wore the leg brace snarled. "Let him talk. When he is finished, we take him."

They walked into the home and sat in their chairs. "Mr. Victorio," one of the harvesters said. "It appears you have some things on your mind and you want to talk. We will listen."

Marriage

Joseph was standing behind his chair when the harvesters returned to enter his home. He was holding a metallic object in his right hand and he placed it in the right pocket of his coat. He sat in his chair and he smiled proudly. "Audrey and I were married."

"Marriage is an archaic and outdated procedure," one of the harvesters said. "Civil unions make more sense."

"In the year 2030, marriage was still accepted among many people," Joseph said proudly. "Do you know the difference between a marriage and a civil union?'

"Sure," one of the harvesters answered. "In a marriage, you are stuck with the person you married for life. In a civil union, vows are repeated every five years. If the couple chooses not to repeat their vows, the civil union is broken. They are free to have a civil union with another person."

"Not quite," Joseph said. "A marriage is a covenant between a man and a woman. The act of marriage establishes a life-long, exclusive relationship. This relationship is different from a civil union as it is a partnership. In this partnership, love is given and received. The purpose of marriage is to form a family to have children. These children are nurtured by the mother and father." He paused slightly. "Of course, a marriage is based on God's plan."

One of the harvesters smiled. "You are stuck together. To dissolve the marriage, you must request and receive a divorce. This is costly. A civil union is more convenient. If things do not work out, in five years, you can select someone else."

"No," Joseph said slowly. "In the Catholic Church, only the Church can dissolve the marriage. It is called an annulment. If the grounds do not meet certain standards, the annulment is not granted. The goal is to work out the problems. In a civil union, there is no effort to work out problems."

"The concept of God is also an archaic concept," one of the harvesters said. "The government does not recognize God. There is only one plan and the government has enacted legislation to follow that plan."

Joseph laughed. "You are comparing the United States Senate with God?"

The harvester who wore the leg brace laughed. "Why not? Like your God, the United States Senate decides who lives and who dies."

"For now!"

"What did you intend by that comment?" one of the harvesters asked angered. "Did you know you could be arrested for that statement? It sounded like you were threatening the entire United States Senate."

Joseph laughed. "I didn't threaten anyone. I just made the comment that, for now, the United States Senate decides who lives and who dies. Is that statement not correct? I just agreed with you. I didn't threaten anyone."

"Sounded like a threat to me," one of the harvesters said. "The statement is true but it was the manner in which you spoke it. It was the manner in which you expressed it."

Joseph shrugged his shoulders and ignored the comments. "In the Catholic Church, an annulment through the nullity process, judges the bonds of marriage, not the parties. It is not a moral judgment. The process only determines if the elements necessary for a valid marriage were present at the time of the wedding."

"In a civil union, the parties are judged not on the bonds of the union but the parties. It is a reversal," Joseph added.

"What are these bonds?" one of the harvesters asked. *That is a weird way to live.*

"Standard things," Joseph answered. "Each person is to accept and fulfill the obligations and rights of the marriage. Each person must have the psychological and physical ability to live a married life as taught by the Church."

"If your wife was a cripple, she should not have married," one of the harvesters said."

Joseph narrowed his eyes. He slowly moved his hand toward the right pocket of his jacket. He could feel the metal object through the cloth of the pocket. His hand moved slowly inward then he removed his hand. "Her damaged leg is not the physical bond the Church looks at. Physical is often seen as an addiction. The addiction could be to some type of drug like alcohol or something stronger. The physical can be related to an inability to conceive children. The marriage vows can be annulled if the party did not disclose this."

"How long does this procedure take?" one of the harvesters asked.

"It could take five to ten years. Sometimes, it is not granted," Joseph answered.

"Civil unions are less expensive and those types of things you mentioned are included in the agreement," one of the harvesters said.

"It is more complicated that that," Joseph said. "If the couple has been baptized, the marriage is seen as a sacrament, a devotion to God and the laws of God and the teachings of the Church."

One of the harvesters looked at the harvester sitting beside him. "I have not been baptized. Have you?"

"I have never been to a church," the harvester answered. "Sundays were a day of rest. I slept late and enjoyed my time off."

"It is more complicated than that," Joseph said.

"How complicated?" one of the harvesters asked. "If you lied before you got married, it is over. Nothing complicated about that."

Joseph smiled slightly. "For those who take their wedding vows seriously, the marriage can only be ended by death!"

Two of the harvesters stood. "What did you mean by that comment?" one of the two yelled.

"Statement of fact," Joseph answered. "In a Church sanctioned marriage, the only thing that can separate the husband and wife is death!"

"Then your marriage to your wife is over," one of the standing harvesters said. "She has been harvested. You are free to select another."

Joseph stood slowly. His eyes glanced at the six harvesters. Two were standing and four were sitting. Three looked like they had concealed stunners. He carefully judged distance, anticipating, which harvester would move towards him first. He looked at the woman who wore the leg brace, she would be last. His right hand touched his right pocket. He could feel the metal object through the cloth. *The two standing are too close. They would move too fast.* He slowly sat in his chair. "You are correct. Audrey has been harvested. According to the Church, she and I fulfilled our marriage vows." He lowered his head. "I am free to select another."

The two harvesters sat in their chairs. "You had three years, didn't you know anyone?" one of the two asked."

Joseph raised his head. "Just because I am free does not mean I am willing. I loved my wife in life and in death. I could not enter another marriage. That is one of the bonds, a full love that I can not give."

"Are you a Catholic?" one of the harvesters asked. "That religion died out more than thirty years ago. They all died out. There were not enough people attending regularly to financially support them."

"No," Joseph answered sadly. "Audrey and I were not Catholic. We were married in a religious ceremony."

"That makes no sense," one of the harvesters said. "You quote the Catholic Church but you are not a Catholic."

"Correct," Joseph said. "However, the Catholic Church is slowly making a come back. There are a few Catholic Churches opening. As we began to age, we started looking for answers. We could not find those answers in the government … we found them in God and the teachings of the Church."

"What questions? What answers?" the harvester who wore the leg brace asked. She seemed interested in what he was saying. He wasn't making any sense until now.

"Life and death," Joseph answered. "Why do we live and why do we die? How can a person judge their quality of life over their quantity of life?"

"Are those the questions?" one of the harvesters asked puzzled. "What are the answers?"

"Faith," Joseph answered. "Faith that there is a higher power a person must answer too." He snarled. "That higher power is not the United States Senate!"

"It is for you," one of the harvesters said. "Your life is over! Your living credits have been set to zero and your name has been removed from the United States' government population database." He laughed slightly. "Mr. Joseph Victorio, as of today, you no longer exist in more ways than one."

Joseph looked puzzled. "When did that happen?"

The harvester laughed. "It has not happened yet." He looked at his wrist watch. "You have twenty minutes before all of your records are erased."

Joseph stood slowly. He walked toward the door and turned. The six harvesters were watching him as he stood and walked toward the closed door. They were looking at him intently. One of the harvesters had reached into his coat pocket and appeared to be holding an object. *He is holding a stunner.* "How?"

The harvester who wore the leg brace held upward a communicator. She pointed to a flashing light and a small button near the flashing light. "This button sends a signal. I will press it once you have been harvested. The person on the other end will manually erase all of your records. Once your records have been erased, they can never be recovered."

One of the harvesters shrugged his shoulders. "It is like an execution at a prison. When the person is executed a signal is sent. The person on the other end receives the signal and erases the records. That person then waits for the next signal."

Joseph looked puzzled. He looked at the device and the flashing light. "What other signal?"

"Four more today, after you, and the system is programmed for every person scheduled to be harvested this week," the harvester who wore the leg brace answered. "This system has more than four hundred names, addresses and scheduled times of harvesting."

Joseph's eyes widened. What she said upset him. "You are going to harvest more than four hundred people this week?"

"Not this week," the harvester who wore the leg brace answered. "It will take some time. It all depends on our schedule." Her eyes glared at him. "Some people accept the government's mandate without question."

Joseph was visibly upset. He walked quickly to his chair and sat down. When he sat down, he sat down very hard. The chair made a noise from his weight and slid slightly backwards. The force of his setting moved his chair backwards more than six feet. Joseph calculated the distance. *Twelve feet! They don't have a chance.* There was more than twelve feet between his chair and the chairs of the six harvesters. He moved his right hand toward the metal object in his right coat pocket. *Not yet. I need more information.*

"What do you mean, erased?" he asked, as he lowered his head. "What do you mean, it can never be recovered?"

"Erased," one of the harvesters answered. He had a slight smile on his face. "Government mandate of records. Once your data file has been erased, there is no way to recover it. There is no way to trace who has been harvested and when."

Joseph slowly raised his head. There were tears in his eyes. "Audrey?" he asked with a pitiful voice. His lips quivered. "There is no record of her life and no record of her death?"

One of the harvesters stood. "Nothing," he answered. "There is no record that Mrs. Audrey Victorio ever lived or died. What was her maiden name?"

"Allison," Joseph answered. "Her maiden name was Audrey Margaret Allison."

"Gone too," the harvester said. He stretched his legs and his arms. He leaned backwards and stretched his neck. "All of the records are complete and they are joined by the government population database. Every record that had her name, every record of her medical treatments, every record of her birth and education, are gone!"

Joseph looked puzzled. "There must be something? She has two daughters?"

"Gone," the harvester answered. He completed stretching and sat in his chair. "The current records on your two daughters do not show who their mother was. Once you have been harvested, their birth records will show no parents."

Careful. Act stupid. He pointed towards the communicator. "There are hundreds of people waiting for your signal?" Joseph asked slowly, carefully.

"Just one," one of the harvesters answered. "There is only one person who controls the government database."

"Is this person the Speaker of the Senate?" Joseph asked.

The harvesters laughed. "No," one of the six answered. "Mr. Speaker is too busy to deal with such trivial things as who lives and who dies. The government database is not located in Washington D.C."

"Nebraska?" Joseph asked puzzled.

The six harvesters laughed. "Why would the government database be in Nebraska? It is located in Missouri."

"Nebraska?" Joseph asked again. He appeared to be very puzzled.

The harvesters laughed. "Mr. Victorio, you are old, useless and deaf," one of the six said laughing. "The government database is located in St. Louis, Missouri not Nebraska."

"Tampa, Florida?" Joseph asked. "The ten people waiting for your signal are located in the railway station in Tampa, Florida?"

The six harvesters laughed. "Old, old, old. Useless, useless, useless," one of the six laughed. "You can not hear." The harvester stood and walked toward Joseph. "Man! Waiting! Alone! Federal building! Fourth floor! St. Louis! Missouri!" he yelled loudly.

Joseph had a look of fear on his face. He held his hands upward to protect his face. *That is exactly what I wanted and exactly what we needed.*

The harvester laughed as he saw Joseph was afraid. He walked to his chair and sat down.

The six harvesters laughed. They were excited by the fear they presented to this old man.

Lemon Theory

Joseph's eyes showed fear. "You are lemons...," he stammered.

One of the harvesters laughed. "Mr. Victorio, it is a good thing you're scheduled for harvesting today. It is obvious you are a deranged and very ill person." He looked at the five harvesters, they were laughing. "I am not yellow and we are not a citrus fruit!"

The six harvesters laughed. They laughed very hard as several pointed toward Joseph. "Lemons," the harvester who wore the leg brace said laughing. "We are wearing white, not yellow."

The harvester was correct. All harvesters wore uniforms of white. They wore white tops and white bottoms. On their white top was an emblem with the seal of the United States Senate.

Joseph's eyes narrowed. He had fear on his face. He wanted to remove the metal object in his pocket. *Not yet.* "Not a citrus fruit."

"Is there another definition of what a lemon is?" one of the harvesters asked. "I only know of one."

Joseph relaxed his body. He was tense and it was showing. Leaning back in the chair, he frowned slightly. "In the early 1960s, the American city of Detroit built cars."

"One of these cars was called a lemon?" one of the harvesters asked giggling. "You think we are cars?"

The six harvesters laughed. "He is really ill," one said. "He thinks we are American automobiles."

Joseph smiled slightly. "The manufactures produced millions of automobiles. These automobiles were of different makes and models. Occasionally, one or more did not work correctly."

"What was wrong with them?" one of the harvesters asked laughing. "They didn't run."

The five harvesters laughed at the joke.

"Not quite correct," Joseph answered. "There were one or more problems that could not be repaired."

"What was wrong with them?" the harvester who wore the leg brace asked. *What do we have to do with defective American automobiles?*

"No one knew," Joseph answered. He shrugged his shoulders. "They were called lemons and legislation was passed that the owner could return them."

The six harvesters stopped laughing. "What does that have to do with us?" one of the harvesters asked. He looked puzzled at Joseph.

"A Sociologist worked in Criminology," Joseph answered. "He was conducting research on prison populations and the general population. He was attempting to show a correlation in the number of people in a given population and the number of people incarcerated."

"What does that have to do with automobiles?" one of the harvesters asked.

"The correlation of the number of people incarcerated and the population closely matched the statistics on cars manufactured and lemons," Joseph answered.

"Statistics can be made to do, say and prove anything," one of the harvesters said. He shrugged his shoulders. "Close means nothing."

"You are correct," Joseph said. He stood slowly and stretched his legs. "The professor's statistics were close but not close enough to be shown as scientifically accurate."

"His theory was wrong," one of the harvesters said.

"Yes," Joseph said. He sat in his chair. "He checked the populations of several countries and he went backwards many years. He was attempting to prove that there was a correlation between people incarcerated and the general population. The numbers were close but they were inconsistent. One countries statistics were different from another countries statistics. The numbers changed based on the year."

"What happened to his theory?" one of the harvesters asked.

"When it was published, the American government arrested him," Joseph answered. "He was fired from his job at the university and disappeared. No one knows what happened to him."

The harvester who wore the leg brace looked confused. "If his theory was wrong, why was he arrested? What interest did the United States government have in a flawed theory?"

Joseph stood again and stretched his legs. He slowly sat in his chair. As he sat down, he pushed his chair further backward. "His theory was that there was a correlation in the number of automobiles produced in the American city of Detroit and the general population. A certain percentage of automobiles were defective. They were made with the same parts. They were made by the same people. They looked the same. For some reason, some of the cars did not work correctly. They could not be repaired. Those defective cars were destroyed."

"His theory was called the Lemon Theory. The professor wanted to prove, scientifically, that the same thing occurred in society. Out of millions of children born, some were defective, they did not work correctly. They were lemons!"

"He was wrong!" one of the harvesters said.

"What was he attempting to prove?" one of the harvesters asked. He was curious. What Mr. Victorio was saying interested him.

"Many people are born with defects," one of the harvesters said. "He wasted time and money." He looked at the five harvesters. "He was arrested because he wasted money on a worthless theory."

Joseph smiled slightly. "The people he called lemons did not have physical problems. They looked OK and they sounded OK. You could not tell a lemon from any other member of society. However, they did not work correctly."

"What was wrong with them?" the harvester who was interested in what Joseph was saying asked.

"They did not seem to learn," Joseph answered. "They seemed normal but they did not have any feelings for anyone or anything."

"They were ignorant?" one of the harvesters asked puzzled.

"No," Joseph answered. "They appeared to be very intelligent. However, they would be arrested many times for the same offense. Some lemons were released from jail and they were arrested again in a matter of hours or days. The criminology theory of the time is that recidivism was a type of socialization. The person had become accustomed to the prison society. They preferred prison over being free."

"That's true," one of the harvesters said. "Many people are imprisoned and they return when they are released. They commit the exact same crime to get a similar sentence. The professor wasted time and money. That theory has been proven many times."

"Perhaps," Joseph said. "His theory was that it was more than that. The lemon preferred prison because they did not have to think for themselves. They were told when to awaken in the morning and when to go to sleep. They did not have to decide what food to eat because it was already decided for them. They could not harm anyone because they were kept from the general population. They did what they were told, when they were told. No questions."

"He could not prove his theory, so what was the problem?" the harvester interested in what Joseph was saying asked.

"For one thing," Joseph answered. "The theory went against common thought. People were different but you could not label them as different. Children, people, with a physical mental defect were called special. Children in school could no longer be separated. The slow student was placed in the same classroom as the exceptional student. Achievement grades were lowered so the special student would not be seen as different. The attempts to solve the labeling problem surfaced many years later as students, with learning difficulties, were graduated. Some students could not do basic math or write a coherent sentence."

"I am confused," one of the harvesters said. "You talk like these people, who have obvious problems, are not lemons. What is a lemon?"

"The professor believed a lemon was a person who had no conscious," Joseph answered. "They had no guilt for anything they did. They followed orders without question."

"He could not prove it," one of the harvesters said. "Why was he arrested?"

Joseph stood. "Simple. What was published was not what he wrote!"

Two of the harvesters stood quickly. "What are you talking about? He couldn't prove it. What was the problem?"

Joseph slowly sat in his chair. He watched as the two harvesters sat in their chairs. As they sat down, Joseph leaned forward and pushed his chair backwards, slowly. "The professor had written his study. The study he had written was that there was no correlation in the automobile lemon and the general population. He was prepared to submit his study, and he had already submitted it for publication, when he had an idea. He obtained a standardized test that was currently in use and he used this test on the prison population. His numbers more closely matched the statistics of the automobile manufactures' lemon statistics."

"What was the test?" one of the harvesters asked.

"A test that was currently in use and this test had been in use for many years," Joseph answered. "The test measured feelings and emotions. The professor discovered that the majority of the prison population had similar scores. However, the results were not consistent with the results and the studies of the automobile industry. There was no statistical support for his theory. He could not prove that there was a correlation in the prison population and the general population. His theory was flawed."

"I am confused," the harvester who wore the leg brace said. "If his theory was flawed, why was he arrested? What was published?"

Joseph smiled. "The theory that was to be published proved no correlation. What was to be published confirmed the existing theories, recidivism was sociological not an effect of a defect. It was an epidemiology study, a comparison of two groups. However, the professor used one additional population. This population was combined with the prison population and the numbers matched. Exactly!"

"What group?" one of the harvesters asked puzzled.

"A similar group to the prison population," Joseph answered. "This group remained in one place for a minimum of two years. He added this group to the prison population and they matched the lemon studies of the automobile manufactures. He reran his basic study and added this group. What he discovered was amazing."

One of the harvesters shrugged his shoulders. "What did he discover?"

Joseph smiled. "The studies of the automobile industry were very exact. They could predict in any given time period, based on the number of automobiles they produced, how many would be lemons. The professor did the same. He used his formula and he could predict the number of people in prison and the other group at any given time. He went backwards in time, and the numbers matched. He looked at other countries, at different times, and the numbers matched. He could accurately predict the prison population and the population of the other group, backward and forward."

The six harvesters looked at Joseph with a curious look.

"The professor had scientifically and statistically proven his theory," Joseph said. "It was when he sent the revised theory to be published that he was arrested by the United States government."

"Why?" one of the harvesters asked puzzled. "If he proved a theory, why was the United States government interested? They should have been grateful for what he discovered."

"No," Joseph said. "The United States government was furious. They did not want people to know what he had discovered. They had already discovered it many years before."

"I have never heard of the lemon theory," one of the harvesters said. He looked toward the others. "If it is true, I would have known."

"Did you take a test for this job?" Joseph asked.

"Yes," the harvester who wore the brace answered. "We all did."

"When did you take the test?" Joseph asked.

"In elementary school," one the harvesters answered. "Do you know this test?"

"Some," Joseph answered. "Question number forty-three. You pass a person who has been injured. Their injury appears to be severe. Do you (A). Help them? (B). Call for an emergency team? (C). Do nothing?"

"C," all six of the harvesters answered simultaneously.

Joseph smiled slightly. "Question number sixty-three. Your best friend lost his job. He comes to you with a request for a small loan. You have the money to loan him. What do you do? (A). Laugh at his problem. It's his problem not yours. (B). Loan him the money and expect him to repay the loan promptly. (C). Loan him the money and tell him he does not have to repay you. You are friends."

"A," all six of the harvesters answered simultaneously.

Joseph narrowed his eyes. He looked at the harvesters, they were proud of their answers. "Question number seventy-three. Your brother is ill and he asks you to come to the clinic to visit him. What do you do? (A). Leave immediately to see him. (B). Wait a period of time. He probably wants something from you. (C). Ignore his request. He probably has some disease that you will catch."

"C," five of the six harvesters answered.

"B," the remaining sixth harvester answered. "My brother always wants something." He looked at the five harvesters. "If he was ill, he would probably ask me to help him, his wife or their two children. It's his problem not mine! It is not my fault that he is ill."

Joseph had a sad look in his eyes.

"Where did that test come from?" one of the harvesters asked. "Those questions sound familiar. Where did the professor get them?"

Joseph frowned. "The test is from the test used by the government to select members of the armed forces. The group the professor added to his study was the number of active members of the United States armed forces. The professor proved that the United States government knew about the automobile manufacture's studies and they had been testing the population and actively recruiting lemons for the service."

All six of the harvesters stood. "You said we were lemons!" one of the six yelled. "What did you mean?"

Careful. They all seemed agitated. "Nothing," Joseph answered. He slowly moved his right hand toward his coat pocket. *They are far enough away.* "There is nothing wrong with being a lemon. It is a very different, special, segment of society. There are degrees of lemons. Not anyone can do what you six do. You should be proud of who you are and what you do. You are proud aren't you?"

The six harvesters looked at each other and sat down in their chairs. "Not really," one of the six answered. "It is a job. It is a living."

The remaining five nodded their heads in agreement.

Joseph moved his right hand away from his coat pocket and casually folded his hands on his lap.

Government

"Government. What government?"

"Your government," one of the six harvesters answered.

"Not mine," Joseph said.

"You question the Senate?" one of the six harvesters asked.

"I question everything," Joseph answered. "This government is not based on the original Constitution. It was altered in the year 2024."

"The Speaker of the Senate has the power to alter anything," one of the six harvesters said. "The Constitution is irrelevant."

One of the six harvesters leaned forward. "Mr. Victorio, these arguments are old and tired. Look around you. The government has given you everything you need. You have shelter, clothing, food and medical care."

"Choice."

"What is choice? If you do not need to make decisions," one of the six harvesters said.

"I want to make my own choices," Joseph said.

One of the six harvesters yawned. The conversation was boring him. "That was once the case, until the people made incorrect decisions. The people could not be trusted to make choices and it was necessary for the government to make those choices for them."

Joseph frowned. "If you are referring to the election of 2024, the people made the correct decision. The government was in shambles with massive debt and the new political party was beginning to make advances until the new party began to dissolve."

"See, you have pointed out the error of the 2024 election," the harvester said. "The people elected a new political party that could not hold its own. As you recall, it was necessary for the Senate to take temporary control of the government."

"Nothing is ever temporary," Joseph said. "As you may recall, the new political party did not dissolve, their leaders disappeared."

"Rumors and innuendo to damage the Senate," one of the six harvesters said.

Joseph laughed. He laughed vary hard. "Rumors and innuendo do not cause members of the House and a new political party to disappear!"

"Unsure times and an unsure new administration," one of the six harvesters said. "No one disappeared, they quit!" He leaned forward. "When they quit, it was necessary for the Senate to temporarily take over the government of the United States."

"Temporary was eighteen years ago," Joseph said. "We have not voted for a president in fifteen years."

"Are you not better off?" one of the six harvesters asked.

"No," Joseph answered. "I want my representatives voted into office, not appointed."

"The government was too large," one of the six harvesters said. "The Senate streamlined the government by combining, the executive, legislative and judicial branches."

"Removing is not combining."

"Combining," one of the six harvesters said irritated. "It was more efficient to combine all three into one governing body. The Senate has done an excellent job of running the United States."

"The Senate ordering the Sergeant at Arms to arrest the president and vice president of the United States is not combining," Joseph said.

The six harvesters looked at each other puzzled.

"Removing the power of each state is not efficient," Joseph added.

"Yes, it is," one of the six harvesters said slowly. He was visibly irritated. "Mr. Victorio, I see no reasoning for what you are saying. If you have a point, make it!"

Joseph stood slowly. He looked at the six harvesters. They were all young, under the age of thirty. They were too young to remember what the United States had once been; a nation of free thinkers and a nation of free speakers. Today, it was ruled by one governing body, the Senate. The Senate had one supreme ruler, the Speaker of the Senate. The speaker held ultimate power and the position was appointed, by members of the Senate, not voted on by the people.

"My point is…," Joseph stammered. "The United States changed when the flag of the United States was removed and replaced by the flag of the Senate."

"So," one of the six harvesters said. He was visibly bored. "What difference does it make which flag flies over the nation's Capitol?"

"It would never have happened if the people had guns!" Joseph yelled.

"Guns were outlawed to protect the people from themselves," one of the harvesters said. "When guns were outlawed, death rates by a means of violence diminished. Abolishing the death penalty decreased the number of violent deaths by the people."

"No it did not," Joseph said. "Deaths increased. The death penalty worked!"

"For whom?" one of the harvesters asked. "When the death penalty was outlawed, deaths lowered. It worked."

"No," Joseph said slowly. "Deaths increased. The death penalty kept the majority of people in line. People like me and many others did not kill for fear of the death penalty."

One of the six harvesters was visibly bored. "Deaths in the population decreased."

"Only from each other," Joseph said. "The death rates continued, rising. The only difference is that the people did not harvest each other, the government began harvesting them."

"Population control has many uses," one of the harvesters said. "Trouble makers were taken care of."

"Members of the House, the president, the vice president and members of the opposing political party were not trouble makers," Joseph said.

"All of this over a flag," one of the harvesters said, amused. He looked at the others. "You did not answer the question. What difference does it make?"

"It means a lot to me and it means a lot to many others," Joseph answered. He had a very sad look on his face."

"Mr. Victorio," one of the six harvesters said. "Who are these others?'

"People like me," Joseph answered. "People who are old enough to remember…what it was once like."

"That is changing," one of the six harvesters said. "There are no people over the age of sixty-five."

"Possibly," Joseph said with a smile on his face. "You do realize that harvesting is not about population control."

"Sure it is," one of the harvesters said with a puzzled look. "There are too many people in the United States and not enough resources, it is necessary to control the population."

"It is not the population the government is seeking to control but memories," Joseph said. "In addition to harvesting lives you are harvesting memories."

"True," one of the six harvesters said. "When you have been harvested, any memory of you will be erased."

"More than that," Joseph said. "In another ten years, there will be no memory of what the United States once was. Anyone who has knowledge will have been harvested. The government's decision of who lives and who dies is not population control; it is an attempt to remove, from the populace, all memories of what once was. The world turned upside down."

"Attempt," one of the six harvesters said. "There is no attempt. Are you ready?"

"No," Joseph answered. "I am not ready." He stood and ran to stand behind his chair.

"I am tired of this," one of the six harvesters said. He stood and pointed his stunner towards Joseph.

Home-Made Weapon

Joseph had run to stand behind his chair where his hands were hidden. His right hand suddenly moved upward. In his hand he held a metallic device.

"What the hell is that?" one of the harvesters asked. His eyes were widely opened. He looked at the small metal device in Joseph's hand. There appeared to be a cylinder type device attached to a handle. A small tube protruded from Mr. Victorio's hand and a small piece of metal, like some type of sighting, was fixed to the top of the metal tube.

"Gun!" Joseph answered laughing. "It's a home-made gun! I made it!"

"Guns were outlawed in the year 2020," one of the harvesters said. He reached for his stunner when the device in Mr. Victorio's hand made a loud pop sound. The harvester was in the process of standing when he was pushed backwards, into the chair. He fell to the floor as a large stain of red appeared on his white coat. The stain quickly expanded as the harvester's body twisted and jerked on the floor. His eyes rolled upward and closed. Then, he stopped twisting and jerking.

"What the hell happened to him?" the harvester who wore the leg brace yelled. She screamed. "He's dead!"

"Not dead," Joseph said. "Harvested. Unfortunately, I did not have time to remove his organs. It doesn't matter."

"That thing works?" one of the harvesters asked quietly. He pointed at the metal device in Joseph's hand. "What struck him?"

Joseph laughed. "What struck him was a bullet. This gun holds nine rounds. Six were used on the harvesters who came for Audrey. I have used it twelve times."

He motioned for the harvesters standing to sit in their chairs and they sat.

Joseph turned slightly toward a door to his left. "Audrey, come out!"

The eyes of the harvesters widened as the door opened and an attractive woman of the age of sixty-eight walked through the door. She walked with a slight limp and moved to stand beside Joseph. In her right hand she held a similar type metallic device.

"How does it feel to lose one of your own?" Mrs. Victorio asked.

"You can't be his wife!" one of the harvesters said. "You were harvested three years ago."

Joseph smiled. "You may have noticed that in the last three years, several teams of harvesters sent to control the population never returned."

"That's true," the harvester who wore the leg brace said. "There have been rumors of harvesters quitting their job. They delivered parts and then quit."

"Those are not rumors," Mrs. Victorio said. "They never returned but they didn't quit. Parts were delivered but those parts did not belong to the person who was to be harvested." She leaned toward Joseph and placed her arm around his shoulder. "We harvested … killed them!"

"Why?" one of the harvesters asked. His eyes widened as he began to rise from his chair.

"Survival!" Joseph answered forcibly. "We were not ready to go. So were several others."

The five harvesters stood and began to reach for their stunners.

The metal device in Joseph's hand jerked five times. With each jerk, a loud pop could be heard. With each loud pop, one of the five remaining harvesters was harvested … killed.

Rescue Mission

Audrey walked to the harvested harvesters and picked up the communicator. A light was flashing. She pressed one of the buttons and the light stopped flashing. Joseph Victorio's name and address were cleared from the display. "You have been erased."

She pressed several buttons and a series of names and addresses were displayed.

"I will contact the others," Joseph said. "Don't press any buttons!"

"I know what to do," Audrey said irritated. She walked through the door to where their desk and personal items were placed. She sat at the desk and began to write the names and addresses displayed.

Joseph followed her into the room. "Who is the most urgent?"

"They are all urgent," Audrey answered. She wrote several names and addresses. "Everyone listed is in bad shape. The government clinics have been withholding medical care and medicine."

"We only have time for one!" Joseph yelled. "A name! Give me a name!"

Audrey looked upward. "This is strange. There is a name on the list that should not be there."

"Why not?" Joseph asked. He walked to the desk and looked at the list of names, addresses and dates she had written. "Which name?"

"This one," she said as she pointed towards a name. "Catherine Meadows. 1956 Pine Way Circle. She is not scheduled to be harvested for eight weeks."

Joseph looked at the name puzzled. "Why would her name be listed if she is not scheduled for eight weeks?"

Audrey frowned. "They are going to harvest her early." She pressed several buttons on the harvester's communicator. The display changed. "According to this information, they have withheld medical treatment from her and denied medication for a period of six months. She is in a very critical condition!"

Joseph removed a device from his coat pocket. He pressed several buttons and spoke into a speaker. "Pick up the cargo at our home and take care of the van. We have an emergency! Catherine Meadows. 1956 Pine Way Circle. Hurry!"

A sound of static could be heard.

"Roger on the pick up. Catherine Meadows. 1956 Pine Way Circle," a woman's voice came from the device. The voice was clear. "We are leaving now!"

A sound of static could be heard.

"We will meet you there," Joseph said.

A sound of static could be heard.

"Do you have any guns ready?" a man's voice asked.

A sound of static could be heard.

"Thirty-two," Joseph answered. "Pick them up with the cargo. There is a list of names and addresses on the desk."

A sound of static could be heard.

"Roger on the additional cargo and names," the man said.

Joseph pressed several buttons and the device went silent.

Two white vans were driven swiftly towards Pine Way Circle. Hammond Burke was driving the first van. Hammond was of African decent. His parents immigrated to America from Ethiopia in the year 1980. He was fifty-seven years old with graying hair. Hammond met Joseph and his wife Audrey when he began to challenge the Speaker of The Senate. His son and wife were killed by the Soldiers of the Senate in a failed revolt and Hammond sought revenge. He heard, through secret channels, that Joseph Victorio was a retired machinist who made guns. He sold everything he owned and approached Joseph to purchase a gun. Hammond was surprised to learn that Joseph and his wife Audrey were descended from immigrants from Spain. When Joseph heard his story, he made him a gun at no charge.

They immediately became friends with one goal; restore America to what she once was. Hammond Burke traveled the southeast, training others to use guns made by Joseph, and recruiting senior citizens for a planned revolt.

He looked to the woman in the passenger seat. "Two more city blocks. Everyone get ready!"

Four men and two women were riding in the back area of the van. They nodded their heads. Two of the four men held a metal battering ram in their hands. The battering ram was used by the harvesters to break down locked doors. The van they were riding in was once used by harvesters. It was theirs now.

The tires of the two vans squealed as a sharp left turn was negotiated from Pine Way Bluff to Pine Way Circle. The vans sped down the street. Hammond counted the unit numbers on the left. "1900, 1912, 1932, 1946, 1952." He slammed on the breaks.

The two vans came to screeching halts and the rear doors opened as men and women quickly exited. They ran to the door of the unit. It was locked!

"Mrs. Meadows!" a woman yelled. "We are friends here to help you! Open the door!"

There was no answer.

Bam! Bam! Bam!

The woman banged on the door with her right fist. "Mrs. Meadows!" the woman's voice was a higher pitch. "We are friends here to help you! Please open the door!"

There was no answer.

"Break it down!" Hammond yelled.

Two men and two women moved towards the door. They swung the battering ram backwards, then forwards.

Bam! Bam!

The force of the battering ram pushed a large indent into the metal door.

Bam! Bam!

The metal door began to buckle at the hinges.

Bam! Bam! Crash!

The metal door was torn from its hinges and crashed to the inside.

The men and women rushed inside. When they entered the unit, they paused. The room was dirty, smelly. They could smell urine and feces.

"Mrs. Meadows!" one of the women yelled. "Do not be afraid! We are not harvesters! We are here to help you! Please answer?"

There was no answer.

"Bedroom!" one of the men yelled.

The men and women rushed to the bedroom. The bedroom door was partially opened. They pushed the door open slowly and entered the bedroom to see it dirty and smelly. A woman lay on the bed. She was partially covered with bed coverings and she appeared to have attempted to leave her bed.

The men and women moved slowly towards the bed. They looked at the woman's face.

Two of the six women screamed.

S.A.A.G.

The white van pulled slowly to the curb. Inside the van six harvesters looked at the home. It was a standard public housing unit. One of the harvesters looked at her communicator. The readout read:

> CATHERINE MEADOWS. 1956 PINE WAY CIRCLE. AGE 65. REQUEST FOR MEDICATION REFUSED FOR A PERIOD OF SIX MONTHS. MEDICAL DENIAL BASED ON PATIENT'S SCHEDULED HARVESTING.

"She is probably dead already," the harvester holding the communicator said. "She has been denied medication for a period of six months."

"What do we do if she is alive and lying in bed?" one of the six harvesters asked.

"I want to stun her," one of the six harvesters said. He reached into his pocket and removed the stunner. "If I place it near her neck, it paralyzes the vocal chords and she will not be able to scream. I like it when their eyes roll and their mouth opens. They are in obvious pain but they can not scream." He squeezed the stunner and a flash of light leapt from the end.

"If she is dead, we can not harvest any organs," one of the six harvesters said.

"They are not using them," one of the six harvesters said. "Most of them are being destroyed. I do not think a request for a transplant has been granted in more than six months. The expense is too high."

"If she is alive, how do we harvest her?" one of the six harvesters asked.

"Smother her," the harvester holding the communicator answered. "Place a plasticized bag over her head while she is asleep."

"We do not have any plasticized bags," the harvester holding the stunner said. "Use a covering from the bed."

The six harvesters nodded their heads in agreement. They exited the van and walked to the small housing unit. On the door was a large sign. The sign was written with a pencil and placed in view.

> WARNING: THE PERSON IN THIS UNIT IS UNDER THE PROTECTION OF S.A.A.G. ENTER AT YOUR OWN RISK.

"Who is SAAG?" one of the harvesters asked puzzled.

"I don't know and I don't care," the harvester holding the stunner said. He reached for the sign and tore it from the door. A small metal bell was attached to the sign and it made a ringing sound. The harvester threw the sign and bell to the side.

"Come in!" a woman's voice said. The voice came from inside the unit. "The door is unlocked! I have been expecting you!"

The six harvesters had puzzled looks on their faces. The woman's voice sounded strong, not weak. The woman's voice sounded pleasant, cheerful.

One of the six harvesters opened the door slowly. They walked inside to see the unit furnished. A woman sat in a chair near the far wall. She appeared to be sixty-five years of age. They expected someone ill, but this woman did not appear ill. She was fully dressed. The clothing she wore was festive; bright colors. In her lap lay a covering. Her hands were under the covering.

The chair the woman was sitting in faced six chairs. The six chairs appeared to be an estimated fourteen feet from the woman. The chairs were made of wood and covered with a cloth that was decorated. The decorations were of extinct animals, small fowl, hare and a deer. The covering had colors of green, red, brown and gold. A clear plasticized covering covered the decorative chair covers.

Underneath the six chairs, on the floor, was a large covering. The covering was cloth and held a design. The design was of a wooded scene. There were many extinct animals, fowl and hare with a reclining deer. Near the reclining deer was her fawn and a large stag appeared to be observant, protecting them. In the background, the sun was rising.

On top of the covering, and under the six chairs, was a clear plasticized sheet. The plasticized sheet covered most of the floor covering.

The walls of the unit were decorated with photographs. The photographs were of several different people. The photographs were of a young child and the child who appeared to have aged. The woman, sitting in the chair, was in several of the photographs mounted on the wall. However, she appeared younger. In one photograph, she held an infant child. In one of the photographs, a male was standing beside her. The woman wore a white dress with a long white headpiece. The man was wearing a black-type suit. He wore a white tie. They were holding hands. In the photograph another man was standing behind him. His right hand embraced their hands and he wore a type of robe that was black. A gold sash draped his robe. In his left hand, he held an opened book. The book had a black cover and was very thick. A large gold cross was in the background.

The unit had a strange appearance. The unit was decorated but there were clear plasticized sheets. The plasticized sheets were attached to the walls, the floor and the ceiling.

The six harvesters were angered at the condition of the unit. Mrs. Meadows was to have given away all of her personal possessions, she didn't. The unit should be bare, it wasn't.

What surprised them more than the decorations, were the six people standing behind the sitting woman. The six people looked older than the woman sitting. There were four men and two women. The men held one of their hands in a coat pocket and the two women held a covering, similar to what the woman sitting, held. The hands of the two women were hidden under the covering.

"Please come in and sit," the woman sitting said. "I have been expecting you. Please sit." Her voice was pleasant and friendly. "Please excuse my home. I did not have time to remove everything." She looked upward at the six people standing behind her. "These are my new friends. They came by to see me off. When I have been harvested, they will remove my personal possessions. Please sit."

The six harvesters walked to the six chairs and sat down. When they sat down, the plasticized coverings on the chairs made a slight noise. They moved their feet and the plasticized covering, under their feet, made a slight noise.

The woman sitting smiled. "My name is Mrs. Catherine Meadows. My married name is Mrs. Matthew Chambers." She looked upward and backward toward the six people standing. "These are my new friends. I would introduce you but I know you are busy and you have many people to harvest today. This won't take long."

The six harvesters looked puzzled. The woman that held the communicator looked puzzled. She looked at the read out again. Mrs. Meadows should be very ill and bed ridden, she wasn't. *Someone screwed up.*

"You know why we are here?" one of the six harvesters asked.

"O yes," Mrs. Meadows answered. Her voice was pleasant and cheerful, almost happy.

Knock. Knock.

Everyone looked towards the door. The door was closed but someone had knocked on the door.

"More new friends," Mrs. Meadows said cheerfully. "I hope you don't mind." She looked towards the door. "The door is unlocked!" she said loudly. "Come in! We are waiting!"

The door opened and six people entered the room. The six people looked older. There were five men and one woman. The five men held one of their hands in a coat pocket and the woman held a covering over her hands, similar to the covering Mrs. Meadows was holding and the covering the two women behind her were holding. The six people entered the room and stood behind the six harvesters. The six people stood far from the six chairs. They appeared to be ten to twelve feet behind the six harvesters.

Mrs. Meadows laughed. "I know why you are here. Before we begin the harvesting, I hope you don't mind my telling a story. I think you will enjoy it."

The six harvesters looked puzzled. The harvester who held the stunner casually placed it in his lap. The woman who held the communicator casually placed it in her lap. Mrs. Meadows could see a flashing light on the communicator. She looked at it puzzled. "Is that it?" she asked one of the six people standing behind her. One of the two women nodded their head.

A loud bang came from underneath the covering Mrs. Meadows held in her lap. The covering jerked upward and fell to the floor. In Mrs. Meadows' hands she held a metallic object. The object appeared to have a cylinder with a handle attached. A hollow tube extended from the cylinder. On top of the tube, there appeared to be a small pointing device.

The metallic object appeared to have smoke come from the hollow tube. The six harvesters were shocked by the noise. Their eyes were widely opened as the woman, who held the communicator, fell forward onto the floor. They watched in amazement as blood appeared to come from the woman's head. The communicator, she held in her lap, made a soft noise as it fell onto the plasticized covering over the decorative floor covering.

The five harvester's eyes widened as they saw each person holding a similar metallic object in their hands.

"I'll take that," one of the twelve people standing said, as he walked from behind Mrs. Meadows. He picked up the communicator and walked towards Mrs. Meadows. She looked at the read out as he pressed a button near the flashing light. The light stopped flashing. "How does it feel to be harvested?"

"I didn't feel a thing," Mrs. Meadows answered.

The man walked to one of the two women standing behind Mrs. Meadows. The woman placed her metallic object in a coat pocket as he handed her the communicator. She pressed several buttons and the read out flashed. The light that stopped flashing began to flash. "Mr. Robert Sanders. 1411 Standherst Drive." She looked upward. "He's in bad shape!"

One of the men standing behind the six harvesters placed the metallic object in his right coat pocket and he reached into his left coat pocket and removed a device. He pressed several buttons and he spoke hurriedly into the device. "Mr. Robert Sanders. 1411 Standherst Drive. According to our information, Mr. Sanders is in a very bad condition. Hurry!"

He pressed several additional buttons on his device. "Sanders! 1411 Standherst Drive! Get the hell out there! Now!"

He pressed several additional buttons on the device. A sound of static came from the device. The harvesters looked puzzled. The man held the device and a sound of static could be heard in the room. Several minutes passed. The man was agitated. He kept pressing buttons and the sound of static was loud and clear in the room. Suddenly, a clear signal was received. "We are here!"

The device in the man's hand made many sounds. There were the voices of many people.

"It's locked!"

"Mr. Sanders! Please open the door! We are friends!"

Pause.

"Mr. Sanders! We are friends here to help you! Please open the door!"

Pause.

"Mr. Sanders! If you are near the door, move away! We are coming in to help you! Move away from the door!"

Rat-tat-tat. Rat-tat-tat.

The sounds were like small explosions.

"It's not working! Get the hinges!"

Rat-tat-tat. Rat-tat-tat.

"It's not working! We are punching holes in the metal door!"

Pause.

"Go through the cement block wall!"

"Mr. Sanders! Get away from the wall! We are coming through the wall to help you!"

Rat-tat-tat. Rat-tat-tat. Rat-tat-tat. Rat-tat-tat. Rat-tat-tat.

The sounds that came from the device were like small loud explosions. There were the sounds of cracking and a noise that sounded like chunks of cement being blown into bits.

Rat-tat-tat. Rat-tat-tat.

"It's working!"

"Bring another one! Hurry!"

Rat-tat-tat-tat-tat-tat-tat. The explosion sounds were coming from more than one direction. The cracking noise of cement was louder.

Rat-tat-tat. Rat-tat-tat.

The sound of large chunks of cement falling, and crashing to the ground, could be heard.

"Holy Moley!"

Rat-tat-tat. Rat-tat-tat.

Cheers erupted from many different voices.

"We are in!"

There were many sounds and many different voices. It sounded like many people running.

"Mr. Sanders! We are not harvesters! We are here to help you! Please answer!"

Pause.

"Bedroom!"

There was a sound like many people running.

"Locked!"

"Break it down!

"No time!"

"Out of the way! Everyone get away from the door!"

"Mr. Sanders! Get away from the door! We are coming through the door!"

Rat-tat-tat.

The sounds from the device were strange. Small explosions, creaking, cracking, splinter sounds; a loud crash.

The device went silent.

A woman's voice could be heard. Her voice was soft but firm, reassuring. "Mr. Sanders. We are your friends. We are here to help you."

There was silence.

The woman's voice rose in pitch and she seemed to be anxious. "Mr. Sanders, are you awake? Don't give up! We are friends!"

The device was silent. Then, there was the sound of a voice. The voice was a man's voice and very weak. "That door was always hard to open. It sticks at the top and sides. Looks like you fixed it. No door!"

Cheers erupted.

Pause.

"Everything is under control!"

The thirteen people in the room smiled but they did not cheer.

"Hammond," a voice came from the device. The voice was male and in a whisper. It was difficult to hear. "There is no food here! He said they cut off his food credits ten days ago. He was scheduled for harvesting."

Pause.

"He has been rationing what he had."

Pause.

"Hammond," a different voice came from the device. This voice was female and also spoken in a whisper. "This isn't working! We have got to find some way to get to them sooner. Mr. Sanders will be OK but the next one may not. They are cutting off their food and medication."

Many sounds and voices could be heard.

"Get the medical condition diagnosis kit and check his vital signs."

"Where is the medical team?"

"What medication was he taking?"

"Feed him, he's hungry!"

The man's eyes blazed in anger as he pressed several buttons and the device went silent. He moved his right hand towards the pocket in his coat. He began to remove the metallic object from his coat pocket when he looked at a man standing behind Mrs. Meadows. The man nodded his head, no. He slowly removed his hand from his pocket. He was upset! He turned quickly, towards the wall, in obvious anger.

The five harvester's eyes were widely opened. They were not sure what they had heard. They heard sounds they had never heard: static, voices, and hundreds perhaps a thousand loud explosions.

They looked at the eleven people in the room who held metallic devices towards them. They looked at the woman, their colleague, who lay motionless on the floor. A large pool of blood had formed around her head. She lay face down and the blood appeared to have come from her face. The blood flowed slowly onto the plasticized cover.

The five harvesters knew not what had happened to her. They didn't know and they didn't care. It didn't happen to them! After they harvested Mrs. Meadows, they would take her with them, a casualty of the job. They were not afraid of the twelve old people standing in the room or the devices they held. They knew something the old people did not know, all five harvesters had stunners. There were five of them. They looked at each other, nodded their heads, and shrugged their shoulders.

Supplications

"My story," Mrs. Meadows continued. She had an expression of sadness on her face. "The last ten years have not been kind to me. I was fifty-five years old in the year 2032. My dear husband had departed three years prior. For reasons I will not discuss, in the year 2032, I reverted to my maiden name and kept the title."

She looked towards her left at the photographs on the wall. "In the year 2032, I really needed my husband but he was not here to help me." She paused. "The time, the event, had come."

She looked at the harvesters. "I attempted to contact people I had known, names I could remember. Gone, all gone," she said sadly. "It was then I realized that I was the only one left."

"I held the one key, but I could not get to it."

"Alone," Mrs. Meadows said. She lowered her head and raised her head. "I was the only one left." She leaned forward in her chair. "I knew this as fact because in the year 2032 nothing happened. I waited and I hoped but nothing happened. I waited as the years began to slip by. Guilt. Much guilt. I was ravaged with guilt."

"What did you do to cause your guilt?" one of the five harvesters asked.

"Nothing," Mrs. Meadows answered. "I did nothing."

"Why did you feel guilty if you had done nothing?" one of the five harvesters asked puzzled.

Mrs. Meadows' eyes began to tear and a tear left her left eye and rolled down her cheek. "I held the key to survival," she answered. "I began to look for people, special people. However, these people were not to be found. I made inquires, discreet comments made in large groups of people. What I needed, I could not get to. What we needed, no one was interested in recovering. Alas, there was no one. In my inability to do something I did nothing. By my doing nothing many people suffered. By my doing nothing, many people would suffer."

"I prayed and I begged. I bargained and I threatened but my prayers were not answered." She shrugged her shoulders. "When I received your letter, I had given up all hope."

"I was not the only one who had given up hope. Everyone had given up hope. I slowly realized when I died the secrets I held would die with me."

Mrs. Meadows composed herself and smiled slightly. "Some people will say, historically, it was fate that brought us together. Some people will say, historically, it was Providence which brought us together." She looked at the people in the room standing. The expression on her face was one of pride and admiration. "It was none of the sort and I will argue with them that say and write such things. It was a miracle."

She leaned forward in her chair. "Do you know why it was a miracle and not fate or Providence?"

The five harvesters had no idea what she was saying. One harvester shrugged his shoulders.

She looked downward and smiled slightly. "It was a miracle in supplication that brought us together. The people, special people, I had been searching for, looking for. A period of ten years I searched for them and I did not find them. When I was on my death bed, unable to walk, unable to stand or unable to speak; all hope had left me. I did not find the people I was searching for and I had run out of time. My time to pass had come."

Mrs. Meadows continued to look downward as she paused to compose herself.

"I had prayed but I am afraid my prayers were selfish in nature. At first I prayed for others. As I aged, I prayed for myself."

Mrs. Meadows leaned forward. Her voice was soft, almost a whisper. "When a person faces their mortality, it is a humbling experience. Lying in my bed alone, all pride had left me. I had been made humble and my prayers became supplications. I prayed not for myself, I prayed for others, many others."

Mrs. Meadows looked upward with a gleam in her eyes. "The miracle is the people I was searching for and I could not find; I did not find them, they found me!"

Mrs. Meadows looked further upward and leaned forward. She composed herself again. "It was most definitely a miracle! They knew nothing about me. Their actions were without regard to payment. Their actions were without concern of who I was or what I could give them. They knew not of what secrets I held."

"They were sent to me in my most desperate of need. They were sent to me in everyone's most desperate of need. The events of the last ten years had made everyone humble. Prayers became supplications."

"A miracle in supplications; soldiers sent by God! Soldiers prepared to battle for me and everyone else."

Mrs. Meadows leaned backwards in her chair and relaxed. She appeared to be upset by the events. She breathed easily and smiled.

One of the five harvesters looked at her. What she had said made no sense. She rambled about some event that occurred in the year 2032. The only event that occurred in the year 2032 was the creation of the Department of Harvesting. All people who attained the legal age of sixty-five were to be harvested. Mrs. Meadows was not sixty-five years of age in 2032; she was fifty-five years of age. She rambled about searching for people and not finding them. Mrs. Meadows claimed she was the only person left who held the key to survival. *What key? Who's survival?* She claimed she had searched for people and the people found her. What she said made no sense. Soldiers sent to her. What soldiers? He had not seen soldiers. Mrs. Meadows was old, useless.

Mrs. Meadows leaned further backwards in her chair. "The information on your device was correct. I would have been dead when you arrived but my new friends, thankfully, arrived more than fourteen days ago. I was in my bed, too weak to move and too weak to prepare food." She pointed towards the door.

The five harvesters looked toward the door. It appeared to have been damaged. Large cracks were in the cement sides and the metal door appeared to be pushed inward, forming a large crater near the center.

"They tore that door off its hinges to get to me!" Mrs. Meadows said loudly.

The eyes of the five harvesters were widely opened as they turned to look at Mrs. Meadows. Her demeanor had changed. Her voice changed. She had spoken softly, quietly. Now, she spoke forcibly. There was fire in her voice!

"They came into my bedroom, pulled me from my bed, and threw me to the floor. They pushed on my chest and forced food and water into my mouth." She pointed toward one of the women standing behind her. "She slapped me!"

The eyes of the five harvesters were widely opened.

Mrs. Meadows looked at the woman standing behind her. Her expression was not one of anger but an expression of gratitude and admiration. "She slapped me! She screamed at me! She yelled for me not to give up! She yelled for me to have faith and hope! My friends!"

Mrs. Meadows smiled. "They threw me in cold water when my fever was high. They forced food and water down my throat! She slapped me! My friends!"

"I yelled and screamed. I was so ill I wanted to die but they would not let me."

The eyes of the five harvesters were widely opened as they listened to her.

"They pulled me from my bed and they forced me to stand and walk. My friends!"

The five harvesters looked towards each other.

"They gave me medicine. Do you know where they got it?" she yelled to the five harvesters.

The five harvesters did not answer. Their eyes were widely opened. Mrs. Meadows' voice was strong, filled with fire.

"My friends have friends," Mrs. Meadows said proudly, answering her own question. "Each one of their friends gave me one pill. That doesn't sound like much, one pill. If you have one hundred people donate one pill; that is one hundred pills."

The five harvesters looked at each other.

Mrs. Meadows smiled. "It took several days but I began to get better. My friends cleaned my home, prepared my meals and arranged my photographs." She pointed toward the wall. "That is my dearly departed husband Matthew," she said proudly. "That photograph was taken the day we were married. That infant in my arms is our son Jacob."

The five harvesters did not look toward the wall they looked at the metal object Mrs. Meadows held. When she spoke, she casually moved the object in her hand from side to side. She pointed the object towards them. She appeared to be moving it from chair to chair, left to right and right to left.

"I did not give up," Mrs. Meadows said. "When I was better, I repaid them."

One of the five harvesters had a puzzled look on his face. "Repaid?"

Mrs. Meadows held the object she was holding upward. "Not a bad job," she said. She turned the object in several directions. When she moved the tube toward the five harvesters, they ducked their heads.

"I know all about guns. When I fired one I noticed it did not sound right. There should have been a loud bang but I only heard a pop."

"Pop?" one of the five harvesters asked.

"Pop," Mrs. Meadows answered. "Not enough gunpowder." She continued to rotate the metal object in her hand. "They didn't have enough gunpowder, so they divided it up. I told them it is better to have fifty bullets that work correctly than four hundred that do not work correctly."

"Four hundred?" one of the five harvesters asked.

Mrs. Meadows leaned forward in her chair. "If there is not enough gunpowder, the bullet travels at a slower speed and leaves lead shavings in the barrel. If there is not enough gunpowder, the powder does not burn at a high enough temperature and the residue clogs the cylinder. They checked their guns and I was correct! Many of the barrels were filled with lead shavings and the gunpowder had begun to eat into the metal."

She held the object in her hand upwards. "The barrel is only four inches in length and it has no rifling. The accuracy is diminished by the length of the barrel and the speed of the bullet. They are only accurate from a distance of ten to twelve feet."

"Guns?" one of the five harvesters asked.

"I know all about guns," Mrs. Meadows said, with a smug look on her face. "My father was afraid of the government.

He began to collect guns in the year 1986. In the year 2020, the government began to confiscate legal guns. My father told us when the government takes away your gun; they have taken away your liberty. The government will begin to decide who lives and who dies."

Mrs. Meadows leaned backwards then she leaned forward. "My father was crazy," she whispered.

"Crazy?" one of the five harvesters asked.

"Crazy," Mrs. Meadows answered. "He collected guns and he forced all of us to learn how to shoot them." She leaned backwards in her chair. "He made us learn how to load them and he taught us how to repair them. My father told us one day this gun will save your life or this gun will save the life of one of your friends."

"Repair?" one of the five harvesters asked.

"Repair them, make bullets for them, shoot them, clean them," Mrs. Meadows answered. She laughed slightly. "My father was crazy! He collected guns, lots of guns. He collected gunpowder and bullets. He had four or five of everything. He had schematics on how to repair them and he had tools to repair them." She leaned forward in her chair. "My father was crazy," she whispered. "He had a chopper!"

"Chopper?" one of the five harvesters asked.

"Chopper, annihilator, trench broom, Chicago typewriter," Mrs. Meadows answered. "My father had a Thompson submachine gun! It had the drum magazine not the stick magazine. That gun could fire one thousand two hundred .45 caliber rounds a minute. The bullets traveled at a speed of nine hundred fifty feet per second and the accuracy was more than one hundred yards."

"One thousand two hundred?" two of the five harvesters asked.

"One hundred yards?" one of the five harvesters asked.

"Nine hundred fifty feet?" one of the five harvesters asked.

"Annihilator?" one of the five harvesters asked.

"I fired it!" Mrs. Meadows said proudly. "It had a kick!" She pointed towards the door. "That chopper could cut through that metal door like a hot knife through butter."

The five harvesters looked towards the door. They could imagine more than one hundred small holes appearing on the inside of the door in a speed of five seconds. They turned their heads towards Mrs. Meadows. Their eyes, that were widened, widened further.

"My father was crazy," Mrs. Meadows said, in a whisper. "He was afraid of the United States government and he bought guns. He taught us how to shoot them and he taught us how to repair them. My father had a chopper. He told us that when the government takes away your gun; they have taken away your liberty. The government will decide who lives and who dies. One day, these guns will save your life or the life of your friends."

"Guns?" four of the five harvesters asked.

Mrs. Meadows smiled slightly. "I told you my father was crazy! He collected guns and he hid them. He hid them where only we could find them. He hid them so I could get to them when I needed them. Well, I needed one!"

"I needed someone to collect them and I repaid my friends' kindness with guns, real guns; I told my friends where my father hid them!"

"Hid?" one of the five harvesters asked. "They work?"

Mrs. Meadows smiled as she leaned backwards towards one of the men standing behind her. "Mr. Joseph Victorio, partial inventory for our guests?"

Joseph smiled. "Nine hundred seventy-two hand guns of various sizes. Three hundred and ninety-four rifles with scopes. Various tools, repair manuals, gunpowder, re-load devices, primers, bullets and shell casings."

Mrs. Meadows smiled. "I left the best for last. Mr. Victorio, how many choppers?"

"Ten cases of one hundred forty-four," Joseph answered. "They are in perfect condition, packed in a heavy lubricant. We tested them! There is enough fire power in four of those choppers to take out a battalion of the military. It took us three days to move the ammunition."

Mrs. Meadows laughed. "I told you my father was crazy. He told us when the government sent the military to get us; he was going to take one thousand with him!"

"Four?" one of the five harvesters asked.

"Battalion?" one of the five harvesters asked.

"Move?" one of the five harvesters asked.

"Move," Joseph answered. "We needed six vans just to move the ammunition." He reached into his left coat pocket and he removed a communicator used by the harvesters.

The harvesters looked about the room as the eleven people standing reached into one of their coat pockets and removed a communicator used by the harvesters. They held the communicators upwards, there were no lights flashing. The information in the communicators had been used and drained.

The harvester who held the stunner in his lap looked confused. *How did they get communicators? Only harvesters have them.*

The five harvesters were numbed by the information they had received.

The Sons of Liberty

Mrs. Meadows laughed. "I told you my father was crazy. He had friends and they were crazy too."

"Friends, crazy friends?" one of the five harvesters asked.

"Quite crazy," Mrs. Meadows answered. "The proper word to use at the time was insane, but they were crazy."

"Insane?" one of the five harvesters asked.

"Very much so," Mrs. Meadows answered. "You should have seen them: walking around in funny costumes, secret handshakes; secret words. Large trucks arriving in the middle of the night to deliver guns. Large trucks arriving in the middle of the night to pick up guns."

"Large trucks?" one of the five harvesters asked.

"They called themselves the Sons of Liberty," Mrs. Meadows said. "Patriots. Protectors of the Constitution. My father said patriots were the backbone and bulwark of America's greatness from the very beginning. Patriots! They were no such thing. They were Masons!"

"Masons?" one of the five harvesters asked.

"Not really," Mrs. Meadows answered. "They were Masons but they had some type of argument and the organization split. My father and his friends were called grannies. The others were called progressives. I don't know the difference and my father never said what the difference was. All I knew is that the Masons split and the grannies began to purchase and hide guns. What guns they could not purchase, they stole. What guns they could not purchase or steal, they made."

The five harvesters looked at each other. They had puzzled looks on their faces. "How many patriots were there?" one of the five asked.

"I have no idea," Mrs. Meadows answered. "They were all over the United States and in every city and every state. We lived on a farm and I recall that there was some type of secret meeting and more than seven thousand men and women came."

"Women?" one of the harvesters asked.

"Women," Mrs. Meadows answered. "Everyone had a specialty. They traded guns and my father was the only one who made choppers. He made choppers and traded them for other guns." She laughed. "My father made them from bare metal. I recall seeing him at work making choppers. On the wall of his workshop were hundreds of Chicago pianos."

"Hundreds?" one of the five harvesters asked.

"Bare metal?" one of the five harvesters asked.

"Workshop?" one of the five harvesters asked.

"Not really a workshop," Mrs. Meadows answered. "It was a factory. My father had more than ten people working with him. He and his friends made Chicago pianos." She paused and smiled slyly. "They made thousands and thousands of Chicago pianos."

The five harvesters looked at each other.

"My father and his friends were insane, crazy," Mrs. Meadows said laughing. "But he and his friends had a sense of humor. Their Chicago pianos had the drum magazine and on the front of each drum magazine he and his friends made, they painted the letters S O L."

"Sons of Liberty. S O L," one of the five harvesters said. "That's funny?"

Mrs. Meadows laughed and the twelve people standing in the room laughed.

"S O L had a different meaning at that time," one of the twelve standing said.

"What meaning?" one of the five harvesters asked.

Mrs. Meadows laughed. "My father and his friends painted the letters S O L on the front of the drum magazine. The only way you could see it is if you were standing directly in front of it. If you were standing directly in front of it, it meant someone was pointing a Chicago piano at you. If someone was pointing a Chicago piano at you, you were S O L – Shit Outa Luck."

"S O L," one of the five harvesters said, confused. "I do not understand what that means."

Mrs. Meadows laughed. "My father said the Chicago piano played a sweet tune to the person who was holding it and a deadly dirge to the person standing in front of it." She leaned forward and whispered. "The Sons of Liberty were insane, crazy. They hid guns, food and medicine." She leaned upwards and smiled smugly. "I know where every cache of guns, food and medicine are hidden. My father left me a map with their secret codes. The codes tell the location of every cache, in every city, in every state."

"Map?" one of the five harvesters asked.

"Not really a map," Mrs. Meadows answered. "It is a code that is hidden in every hidden cache. My father taught me all of the codes. If you locate one cache and know the codes, it tells you where other caches are hidden." She looked upward at the people standing behind her. "One of my gifts to repay my new friends was how to use the codes."

"Food?" one of the five harvesters asked. "What kind of food?"

"A terrible tasting food," Mrs. Meadows answered. "Something called freeze dried. You mix it with water."

"Water?" one of the harvesters asked. He became excited and his eyes widened even further. "You know where to find water?"

"Yes," Mrs. Meadows answered. "It tastes stale. You have to put pills in it before you drink it."

The five harvesters looked puzzled. "Why would people hide guns, food, medicine and water?" one of the five harvesters asked.

"They were afraid of what the government, one day, would do," Joseph Victorio answered.

A cloud of silence fell about the room.

"Crazy," one of the five harvesters said. "The Sons of Liberty were crazy. The government has done nothing wrong."

The Harvesting

"I almost forgot my original story," Mrs. Meadows said. She placed the metallic object in her hand to her side. She reached behind her, near her waist area, and removed what appeared to be an object three times the size of the one she held. This object was different. The one she had held was small and the color was a dull bluish gray. This object was a bright silver color.

Her voice was calm and emotionless. ".357 stainless steel magnum."

Mrs. Meadows' voice and manner changed again. The eyes of the five harvesters were widely opened, when they saw the object she was holding, their eyes opened wider.

"My story," Mrs. Meadows said. She held the first object with one hand but now, she held the second object with two hands. "Many years ago, people hunted fowl, hare and deer. They were called hunters. Some people did not like the term hunting and it was changed to harvesting. The hunters no longer hunted the animals, they harvested them. The harvesters came into their homes, the woods and meadows, and they harvested them to control the population. The animals were defenseless. I always wondered what would have happened if the small animals had weapons similar to the harvesters. I always wondered what would have happened if the events were reversed."

Mrs. Meadows smiled. "What would happen if the harvesters did not have weapons and the defenseless animals had weapons?"

She smiled slightly as she pointed the metallic device in her hands towards the harvester who held the stunner in his lap. She spoke to the remaining four but her eyes and her manner seemed to be directed toward the harvester, who held the stunner in his lap.

"You read my sign, but you ignored it. It is like a hunting sign; a warning sign. You chose to ignore my warning. This home is protected by S.A.A.G. That means Seniors Armed Against Government mandated population control. I am afraid you have entered very dangerous woods and the defenseless are no longer defenseless."

Mrs. Meadows smiled. Her eyes never moved from the harvester who held the stunner in his lap. Her face showed no emotion as she stared into his eyes.

One of the harvesters looked at Mrs. Meadows and he looked at the harvester who held the stunner in his lap. Her words had been deliberate, calculated and aimed at him and him alone. He looked at Mrs. Meadows and the object she held in both hands.

Her voice and manner had changed, again. At first, she appeared to be old, weak and defenseless. Her stories seemed irrational, without meaning and out of context with the current event. Often, she repeated herself. He slowly realized her stories and manner of speaking was a trick! Her manner of speaking placed the harvesters into a false sense of security.

He looked upward at the people in the room and the objects they held in their hands. He looked downward at the harvester lying in the floor, she was not moving and a large puddle of her blood was on the plasticized covering.

He looked at the object Mrs. Meadows held in both of her hands. It was pointed towards them. Her stare was cold, deadly. The harvester became afraid. *What has she been saying? Something about hidden guns, maps, codes, and soldiers.* For the first time in his life, he was afraid, very afraid.

The harvester holding the stunner in his lap did not seem to notice that she appeared to be speaking to him. He showed no emotion in his face and he looked at her with a puzzled look, he had no idea what she was saying.

"The story does have a happy ending; the harvesters become the harvested."

She placed her right thumb on a lever attached to the cylinder and pulled her right thumb backwards. The five harvesters heard a click sound as the cylinder rotated toward their left.

The six people standing behind the harvesters quickly separated when Mrs. Meadows changed her sitting position. They moved away from behind the six chairs.

The harvester, who was afraid, quickly stood when Mrs. Meadows stood. Words flashed through his mind. *I know where every cache of guns, food and medicine are hidden. I needed someone to collect them and I repaid my friends' kindness with guns, real guns. I told my friends where my father hid them! My father taught me all of the codes. If you locate one cache, it tells you where the others are hidden. A miracle in supplications; soldiers sent by God! Soldiers prepared to battle for me and everyone else.*

Words flashed through his mind from the morning meeting. *We have received reports from all over the United States that harvesters are quitting! We can't find them! When did you receive the reports? They began two days ago. The reports began in Boston, Massachusetts. Then we received reports from Nevada, Kentucky, California, Texas and Maine. This morning, I received more than two hundred reports of teams of harvesters missing: North and South Carolina, New York, Hawaii, Alaska, Vermont, Kansas, Ohio, Tennessee, Georgia, Alabama and Florida. Something is happening!*

He looked at the harvester lying on the floor. *The story does have a happy ending; the harvesters become the harvested.*

Mrs. Meadows' expression changed. Her smile turned into a snarl. The expression on her face was one of anger, revenge. The harvester finally understood what she had been saying. *Guns! Hidden guns! These people have real guns!* He quickly reached for his stunner as the three harvesters stood and began to remove their stunners from their jacket pockets. The harvester, sitting in the chair, looked puzzled when he saw the three harvesters stand. The four harvesters standing held their stunners upwards as he leaned forward to grab the stunner in his lap.

Twelve loud bangs erupted from various parts of the room.

One loud boom erupted from the hollow tube on the object Mrs. Meadows held in both of her hands. The wooden seat back of the chair the harvester was sitting in burst apart as the wall behind him exploded! A large chunk of cement was torn from the wall, leaving a seven inch deep, eighteen inch wide, gapping hole in the cement block.

The harvester's chair overturned and he was thrown backwards more than six feet from the chair he was sitting in. His lifeless body rested on the floor, face upward, with a hole through his heart. The harvester's blood, from the chest wound, was on the clear plasticized sheets attached to the ceiling, walls and floor of the unit.

Mrs. Meadows was not sitting in the chair she was standing, holding the metal object in both hands. The bullet fired with such force, the object in her hands jerked upwards, above her head. A thin trail of white smoke came from the opening of the stainless steel barrel; the friction of the bullet heating the lubricant in the barrel created the white smoke.

She slowly lowered the object in her hands and looked at the six bodies. *One day, this gun will save your life. Use it without regret. Use it without remorse.*

Mrs. Meadows cleaned the object, her father's favorite gun, before the harvesters arrived. Before the harvesters arrived she prepared special shells, load, her father's favorite.

"Wad cutter!"

Government Population Database

Charles Manners sat at the computer terminal on the fourth floor of the federal building in downtown St. Louis, Missouri. He was deleting the names and data of people who have been harvested. Charles had entered more than two hundred names when he paused. He heard noises, strange noises.

Bam! Bam! Bam!

Crash!

Zing. Zing.

Rat tat-tat. Rat tat-tat.

Boom! Boom!

The noises he heard were faint. He stood from his seat and walked to the door. He looked out the peephole in the door and the hallway was clear. Charles typed his exit number on the keypad and opened the door. The hallway was clear. He walked into the hallway near the elevators and stairwell and listened.

He listened for more noises but he did not hear anything. He walked into the computer room and closed the door.

Charles sat at his keyboard and he began to enter the name Silkie Sanchez when he noticed one of the camera monitors was black. There were several camera monitors near the computer terminal. The camera monitor that displayed the main entrance was black. Four armed soldiers of the Senate, with stunners, guarded the front entrance. The camera was black and did not display the front entrance.

He looked at several monitors. The monitors displayed several sections of the front, side and rear entrances to the federal building. As he looked at the cameras, they became black. He looked at his wrist watch, 6:19 P.M.

Charles paused. "Electrical failure".

He stood and walked to the computer system. He checked to see if the emergency power system had activated, it didn't. Puzzled, he sat in his chair.

Charles heard more faint noises. The sound was like doors opening and closing and many people running. He walked to the door and looked out the peephole. The peephole was black. He could not see the hallway.

Knock! Knock! Knock!

"Delivery," a woman's voice said.

"You are early," Charles said as he typed his exit code on the keypad. He opened the door to see the hallway filled with old men and old women. The people held sticks in their hands. Many of the sticks had a round drum on the front with the letters S O L painted on the drum.

The door was pushed inward from the outside forcing Charles to move backwards.

"Don't let him touch the terminal!" a woman's voice yelled.

Charles turned and ran towards the terminal. He stopped at the keyboard and removed a stunner from his pocket. He pointed it towards the people in the doorway and squeezed it.

Zing.

A flash of light leapt from the end of the stunner extending to a distance of three feet. The flash of light was bright, intense.

Boom! Boom! Boom!

Three bullets struck Charles in his chest and he was thrown backwards to the floor of the computer room. The room suddenly filled with old men and old women.

"Don't touch anything!" a woman's voice yelled.

Dr. Heylen ran to the computer terminal and she began to type commands on the keyboard. "IMS!" she yelled. "Who knows IMS?"

Three women in the large group of people raised their hands.

Dr. Heylen motioned for them to come forward as she stood. The three women ran to the computer terminal. One woman sat in the seat and she began to type commands.

"Do not touch anything!" Hammond Burke yelled. "What do we have?"

Two men were examining boxes near the computer system. "Standard backup units," one of the two men answered. "We do not have the equipment here to copy their data."

"Answers! I need answers!" Hammond yelled.

"Transfer the backed up data to the university computer!" one of the two women near the terminal yelled.

"Transferring now!" the woman sitting at the terminal yelled.

"Time? I need the time?" Hammond yelled.

"A minimum of two hours to transfer the backed up data!" the woman at the terminal answered.

"Can't do it!" Hammond yelled. "We have to be out of here in twenty minutes."

"It will work," Dr. Heylen said. "The university computer has enough storage for the data. It will take them more than four hours to get into this room."

"How do we fix it?" Hammond yelled.

"Simple," the woman typing on the keyboard answered. "I can delete the date of birth field on the database structure."

"What will that do?" Hammond yelled.

"It will delete every date of birth of every person in the United States," Dr. Haylen answered. "They will not know when a person attains the age of sixty-five."

"Do it!" Hammond ordered.

"Done!" the woman sitting at the computer monitor yelled.

"Out of here!" Hammond yelled. "Take him and clean up!"

Several people picked up the body of Charles as many people began to clean the blood from the floor.

"Erasure and backup programmed to begin in two hours fifteen minutes!" the woman sitting at the computer terminal yelled. "It will delete any backup stored and backup existing data that does not have the date of birth field."

Dr. Heylen looked at the computer desk. On the desk was a list of names printed on paper. The people listed were harvested. She picked the papers upward and turned toward Hammond. "What do we do with these?"

"Nothing," Hammond answered, as he shook his head. "We have to leave them. We can not take anything with us because we can not raise suspicion." He slowly lowered his head. "We were too late to save them but we are not too late to save the others."

He quickly raised his head. "Out of here folks! We have names and addresses! We have people to save!"

"Not yet!" the woman sitting at the terminal yelled. "Backdoor! We need a backdoor!"

"I can do it!" one of the two women standing yelled.

The woman sitting at the terminal quickly stood as the woman who yelled sat in the seat. The woman began to type commands onto the keyboard.

It seemed like hours but it was only minutes. "Backdoor!" the woman typing on the keyboard yelled. "We have a complete remote control of the government population database!" She typed several commands and the computer terminal displayed a standard entrance screen.

"Move out!" Hammond ordered.

Dr. Heylen slowly replaced the sheets of paper on the computer desk. She wept as she and the people exited the computer room. One of the men activated the door, locking the now empty room, seemingly from inside.

No Warning

Louisville, Kentucky

The white van pulled to the curb slowly and stopped in front of the public housing unit. "Martha Etheridge," one of the six harvesters said. "Her husband is two years younger than she is but we have orders to harvest both of them."

The six harvesters noticed many people exiting their living units. This area was mixed, old and young, single and married. The people who exited the units were younger men and women with children. Several children, under the age of ten, stood with their parents. The people stood looking at the white van.

The six harvesters exited their van. "What are you looking at?" one of the six harvesters yelled. He held his stunner upwards and squeezed it. The flash of light from the stunner was bright, intense. The men and women grabbed their children and ran into their units when they saw the flash.

"You are next!" the harvester holding the stunner yelled. He shook his right fist at the people who had run inside their units. "I am going to get you when you least expect it!" He turned towards two of the male harvesters. "Get the battering ram!" He looked at the two women. "If the door is locked we will break it down! When we break down the door, stun them!"

The two men opened the back door of the van and removed the metal battering ram. They held it as they walked to the unit of Martha Etheridge. The harvesters walked onto a cement porch and paused before the metal door. One of the women attempted to open the door but it was locked from inside.

Bam! Bam! Bam!

One of the six harvesters banged his right fist on the metal door.

"Open the door!" one of the male harvesters yelled.

"Go away!" a woman yelled from inside.

"We have done nothing wrong!" a man yelled from inside. The woman and man's voices were high pitched. They sounded like they were afraid.

"Open this door in the name of the Senate or we will break it down!" one of the male harvesters yelled.

"No!" the man yelled from inside.

The people in the adjoining units slowly opened their doors when they heard the loud voices. They walked cautiously to their cement porches.

"Break it down!" one of the female harvesters ordered. The two female harvesters moved sideways, away from the door.

The four men took hold of the battering ram and swung it backwards then forwards.

Bam!

The force of the battering ram placed a large dent in the metal door.

"Leave us alone!" the woman yelled from inside.

"Help! Help!" the man inside yelled.

The people in the adjoining units stood and watched.

The four men took hold of the battering ram and swung it backwards then forwards.

Bam!

The force of the battering ram deepened the dent in the metal door and one of the door hinges snapped.

"Help! Help!" the man and woman yelled from inside.

The people in the adjoining units stood and watched.

"One more time!" one of the female harvesters yelled. The two women held their stunners upwards and squeezed them. Two flashes of light leapt from the ends of the stunners. The lights were bright, intense. The people standing and watching did not run when they saw the flashes of light; they stood watching, waiting.

The four men took hold of the battering ram as the two women moved to stand in front of the door. The two women prepared to rush inside when the door was broken down. The four men took positions and changed their grip on the battering ram. They swung it backwards.

"Now!" the people standing on their porches screamed.

Rat-tat-tat-tat-tat-tat.

More than one hundred small holes appeared in the metal door. The bullets were fired from inside the unit of Martha Etheridge, through the door. Bullets struck the six harvesters in their chest, arms and legs. Loud pinging noises sounded when the bullets struck the metal battering ram in the hands of the four men, knocking it out of their hands. The force of the bullets pushed all six of them backwards away from the door.

Rat-tat-tat.

The six harvesters' body's jerked as additional bullets came through the metal door and struck them. The number and force of the bullets pushed them backwards and they fell to the cement porch.

Rat-tat-tat.

Bullets blazed through the metal door and struck the white van. Large holes appeared in the side of the van and the glass windows shattered.

Cheers erupted from the people standing in the adjoining units.

The damaged door to the unit was thrown open from inside as an elderly man emerged from the inside holding a Chicago piano.

"SAAG! SAAG!"

The people standing in the adjoining units cheered when they saw the elderly man emerge from the unit.

An elderly woman followed the man. In her hands, she held a shotgun.

"SAAG! SAAG!"

The people standing in the adjoining units cheered when they saw the elderly woman emerge from the unit.

"SAAG! SAAG!"

The elderly man held his left hand upward and the cheering stopped. Everyone became quiet.

The six harvesters lay motionless on the cement porch. The two members of S.A.A.G. approached them cautiously and looked at them carefully. The harvesters were harvested; they had been struck with more than fifty bullets. The elderly woman looked at the people standing in the adjoining units and nodded her head.

"SAAG! SAAG! SAAG!"

Loud cheers erupted from the people.

The elderly woman holding the shotgun reached into her pocket, removed a communicator, and pressed several buttons. "Pickup at the home of Martha and James Etheridge."

"SAAG! SAAG! SAAG!"

Martha and James Etheridge emerged from their unit as their neighbors cheered. They looked at the damaged door and waved to their friends.

"SAAG! SAAG! SAAG!"

People began to emerge from their units when they heard the loud cheers. The neighborhood street in front of the unit of Martha and James Etheridge quickly filled with people.

The Harvesting of Joseph Victorio

"SAAG! SAAG! SAAG!"
Men, women and children cheered.

Tampa, Florida

The white van pulled slowly to the curb. The two harvesters riding in the front seats looked outward. The street and sidewalk was empty. The neighborhood was strangely quiet.

One of the harvesters looked at the communicator and laughed. "Twins! We have two female twins!"

One of the harvesters sitting in the back of the van laughed. "Who?"

"Mary and Jerrie," the harvester answered. "They will be sixty-five years of age in two weeks."

"I have never harvested twins," the harvester sitting in the driver's seat said. "We should do something special. Since they were born at the same time, they should be harvested at the same time."

Several loud laughs could be heard from outside of the van.

"How?" one of the six harvesters asked laughing.

"Set your stunners on low," the driver answered. "We will position them so they can see each other."

The six harvesters removed their stunners and changed the setting from high to low. They squeezed them and a small light, less than six inches, leapt from the ends. The lights were not bright; the lights were more of a quick flicker.

Their loud laughs could be heard from outside the van.

Boom! Boom!

Two bullets smashed through the front windshield striking the two harvesters sitting in their seats.

Rat-tat-tat. Rat-tat-tat.

More than one hundred bullets struck the side of the van from two different directions. The bullets blazed through the metal side of the van, striking the four harvesters sitting in the back seats.

The back door of the van was jerked open from the outside.

Ka-boom! Ka-boom!

The S.A.A.G. member fired both barrels of the shotgun at the six harvesters. The harvesters were already harvested and the blasts from the shotgun tore large holes into the back of the seats.

"SAAG! SAAG!"

Loud cheers erupted as people began to come out of their homes.

"SAAG! SAAG!"

Mary and Jerrie Crawford heard the cheers. They laughed as they opened the door of their home. They hugged each other as they looked at the damaged white van.

"SAAG! SAAG!"

"Pick up at the home of the twins," one of the S.A.A.G. members said into a communicator.

"SAAG! SAAG!

Many people cheered.

San Diego, California

The white van moved casually toward North Main Street. "One old man named d'Artagnan," the female harvester sitting in the front passenger seat laughed. "What a name?"

"One of the Three Musketeers," one of the six harvesters answered laughing. "He may meet us at the door with a sword."

They laughed as the driver turned left from West Main Street to North Main Street. The driver saw something in the road and quickly stopped the van.

Standing in the street was a large number of people.

"All for One and One for All!" the people in the crowd yelled. The people were young and they appeared to be standing in a circle. In the middle of the circle was an elderly man. Four old men stood in front of the crowd holding what appeared to be sticks. A drum was placed towards the front of the sticks and the letters S O L were painted on the drum.

"We will not allow you to harvest Mr. d'Artagnan!" a young woman in the crowd yelled.

"What the hell?" the driver asked puzzled.

The harvester sitting in the front passenger seat became excited. "Run them down with the van!" she yelled. "Run them all down!"

One of the harvesters sitting in the back of the van leaned upward and looked out the front window. "There are young men and women in that crowd."

"Who cares!" the female harvester sitting in the front passenger seat said. "Harvest every person in that crowd! Run them down with the van and stun who ever is left standing! Set stunners on high!"

The four harvesters setting in the back seats removed their stunners, set them on high, and squeezed them.

Zing. Zing.

The flashes of light were bright, intense.

The people standing in the crowd could see the flashes of light inside the van. They did not run when they saw the flashes of light and heard the sound of the flashes. The young people moved closer towards the old man standing in the middle of the circle, forming a barrier to protect him.

The driver pressed his foot on the accelerator. The tires squealed as the rear tires pushed the van to the left and right.

The driver straightened the steering wheel as the van sped towards the crowd of people.

Rat-tat-tat-tat-tat-tat.

Bullets blazed from the four Chicago pianos, striking the van head on. The windshield shattered as bullets punctured the glass. Loud thuds could be heard as bullets struck the grill, front rubber bumper and solid rubber tires. The van swerved towards the right when the two front tires cracked and were thrown from the metal rims.

Rat-tat-tat.

Bullets punched holes in the exposed left side of the van as the van swerved to the left.

Rat-tat-tat-tat-tat.

The van began to slow as bullets blazed into the fenders and engine well, damaging the engine.

The van slowly came to a stop as the four S.A.A.G. members rushed towards it.

Rat-tat-tat-tat.

They pointed and fired their Chicago pianos at the left side of the damaged van. More than three hundred holes appeared on the left side of the van as loud thuds could be heard.

"SAAG! SAAG!"

The people standing in the street cheered.

One of the four S.A.A.G. members approached the rear of the van and fired bullets from his Chicago piano through the rear door.

Rat-tat-tat.

He opened the rear door quickly to see all six of the harvesters harvested.

"Pick up near the home of d'Artagnan LaMont," one of the S.A.A.G. members spoke into the communicator.

"SAAG! SAAG!"

The people standing in the street cheered.

Memphis, Tennessee

The harvester's control room was filled with screaming people as the commander was attempting to regain order. "You are perfectly safe!" he yelled.

"Something is happening!" one of the thirty frightened harvesters yelled. There were five teams in the room.

The door to the control room burst open from the outside as two old men and two old women rushed inside the room. The four old people held sticks in their hands. There was a round drum toward the front with the letters S O L painted on it. "Move away from the door!" one of the two women ordered.

The commander and the harvesters moved backwards away from the door. Angered, they removed their stunners from their coat pockets and squeezed them.

Zing. Zing.

The flashes of light were bright and intense.

The four old people were not frightened by the flashes of light. "Surrender in the name of SAAG!" one of the two old men ordered. "If you want to live, drop your stunners!"

"Old men and old women challenging us with sticks!" the commander laughed. "Set your stunners on high and burn them! Show no mercy! Charge!"

The harvesters set their stunners on high. They held them upward as they rushed toward the four old people.

Zing. Zing.

Rat-tat-tat-tat-tat-tat-tat.

Government Healthcare Decisions

The young man presented his medical prescription and identification card to the dispensing agent at the government healthcare clinic. The agent looked at the prescription curiously.

MAYATAB 5-500 TABLET
TAKE 1 – 2 TABLETS BY MOUTH
EVERY FOUR HOURS AS NEEDED FOR PAIN

QTY – 100
FIVE REFILLS AUTHORIZED
ALL FIVE REFILLS MAY BE DISPENSED AT PATIENT'S REQUEST

"I would like all five refills," the young man said. "I will be traveling and I may not be near a refilling prescription clinic."

The agent nodded her head as she accessed the government population database. She entered the man's name and identification number. The system paused slightly. Then, the information on the young man appeared. His photograph and name matched. She accessed the healthcare section. The system paused slightly. The prescription appeared on the computer screen and matched.

"Excuse me," the agent said. "I will need to verify if we have six hundred." She walked to the rear of the clinic and knocked on the door of the healthcare director.

"Enter," a woman's voice said.

She entered the director's office. "I have an unusual prescription."

The director nodded her head.

"There is a young man who has a prescription but I think the medical diagnosis is incorrect," the agent said.

"Incorrect?" the director asked puzzled.

"Incorrect," the agent answered. "The medication prescribed is the real stuff, not generic."

"What is wrong with it?" the director asked.

"This man is young, under the age of forty," the agent answered. "The medication prescribed is for old people. It is mainly prescribed for arthritis but it can be used for a variety of ailments that only affect the elderly."

The director looked puzzled. "Give him a generic."

"We can't," the agent said. "That is the strange part. The prescription is for the real stuff. Those pills cost eighty dollars each."

The director looked puzzled. "Do we have the medication?"

The agent laughed. "We have thousands. We have not dispensed this brand of medication in more than one year. The Department of Harvesting ordered this type of medication to not be prescribed."

"Why?" the director asked.

"It works," the agent answered. "Denying the medication speeds up harvesting among the elderly."

"Did we receive a direct order from the Department of Harvesting not to dispense this type of medication?" the director asked.

"No," the agent answered. "Only the healthcare agents received the direct order. We only dispense what has been prescribed. We are not authorized to diagnose. We are ordered to follow the healthcare agent's decisions."

The director looked worried. "If this young man has a prescription, we must fill it. It is against government law to challenge a decision made by the healthcare agent. We could go to prison if we questioned it."

"It is incorrect," the agent said. "This young man does not need this medication. It is for old people. I think we should contact the healthcare agent and verify its accuracy."

"I am not going to prison because of a healthcare agent's mistake," the director said. She looked puzzled. "Why would the agent prescribe the real stuff not the generic?"

"The generic doesn't work," the agent answered. "In the year 2036, the Senate began to tax the pharmaceutical companies. They were heavily taxed and they began to substitute generics that were not really generic. Their efforts were to cut costs. All of the real medicine began to be produced in Mexico. The only country that produces real medicine is Mexico."

"Do we have the generic?" the director asked.

"Yes," the agent answered laughing. "We have hundreds of thousands! They do not work. The generic costs one penny for three thousand. If you need real medicine, you have to go to Mexico to get it." She paused. "These pills prescribed were purchased from Mexico."

"Eighty dollars a pill?" the director asked. "How many pills were authorized?"

"Six hundred," the agent answered. "That is forty-eight thousand dollars worth of medicine. At two pills a day, that is a three hundred day supply. At three hundred days, that is enough medication for ten elderly people for one month." She looked towards the door. "That young man doesn't need this medication. Only old people need it."

The director looked frightened. "It could be a trick!"

"Trick?" the agent asked puzzled.

"Trick," the director answered. "It has happened before. Mr. Speaker will send people to a medication dispensing clinic with false prescriptions. One of the directors challenged a prescription and contacted the healthcare agent. The agent was angered that her decision was questioned. She demanded to know who the person was and where they were located."

"What happened?" the agent asked worried.

"The penalty for questioning a healthcare agent's decision is four years in prison or loosing your dispensing license," the director answered. "Within thirty minutes, Soldiers of the Senate arrived at her location. The director was stunned! When she awoke, she was in a prison. No one ever heard from her or saw her again. I think she died in prison for violating Mr. Speaker's order not to question a healthcare agent's decisions."

"Fill it!" the director ordered. She stood. "Do not contact the healthcare agent! I am not going to loose my license or spend four years in prison because I questioned a healthcare agent's decision. It is not my concern that a healthcare agent does not know what they are doing!"

The agent nodded her head and walked to the dispensing area. She filled the prescription and handed the packages to the young man. "I hope you feel better."

"Thank you," the young man said as he turned and walked away.

A young woman was standing behind him and handed two prescriptions and her identification card to the agent.

MAYATAB 5-500 TABLET
TAKE 1 – 2 TABLETS BY MOUTH
EVERY FOUR HOURS AS NEEDED FOR PAIN

QTY – 100
FIVE REFILLS AUTHORIZED
ALL FIVE REFILLS MAY BE DISPENSED AT
PATIENT'S REQUEST

HYDROCHLOROMEXIZIDE 25 MG TABLET
TAKE ONE TABLET BY MOUTH EVERY DAY

QTY – 100
FIVE REFILLS AUTHORIZED
ALL FIVE REFILLS MAY BE DISPENSED AT PATIENT'S REQUEST

The young lady smiled. "I would like all five refills. I am scheduled to travel to another country and I may not have access to a U.S. government healthcare dispensing clinic."

The agent nodded her head as she accessed the government population database. She entered the woman's name and identification number. The system paused slightly. Then, the information on the young woman appeared. Her photograph and name matched. She accessed the healthcare section. The system paused slightly. The prescriptions appeared on the computer screen and matched.

The agent looked at both prescriptions curiously. The Hydrochloromexizide was not generic. It was the real stuff from Mexico! Each pill cost six dollars. Six hundred pills were three thousand six hundred dollars. "How old are you?"

"Thirty-two," the woman answered. "Why?"

The agent frowned. "One of these prescriptions is for an elevated blood pressure. It is normally prescribed for elderly people. Many elderly people over the age of sixty years have an elevated blood pressure."

The young woman smiled. "It is genetic. Both of my maternal grandparents have it."

The agent frowned. "Your grandparents are alive?"

"They were both scheduled to be harvested two weeks ago," the young woman answered sadly. "The event upset me and I went to the government health clinic. Tests discovered I have high blood pressure and other problems."

"You look fine to me," the agent said. She turned to walk towards the director's office when she paused. *I am not going to prison.* She walked to the dispensing area and filled the two prescriptions.

"I hope you feel better," she told the young woman as she handed her the packages.

"Next. How may I help you?" the agent asked a young woman.

The customer looked young, under the age of thirty. "I would like all five refills please," the young woman said as she handed the agent two prescriptions and her identification card.

The agent looked at the line of people standing behind the woman; there were young men and women in the line, under the age of thirty. The people waiting smiled as they held their prescriptions upwards. Many of the people held one and two prescriptions. One young man held four prescriptions.

One young woman held six prescriptions upwards and smiled. "Can I get all five refills today?"

Government Grocery Order

Knock. Knock.

"Enter," a man said.

The door to the government food dispensing manager's office opened. "I have a strange order," the dispensing agent said.

The manager nodded his head.

"We normally dispense a two week supply of food for a family of three but I have an order that is large enough to feed twenty people for one month."

The manager looked puzzled. "What kind of order?"

"It is strange," the agent said. "All of the food is mainly dispensed to the elderly." He handed the food order to the manager.

The manager looked at the order.

TWENTY CASES 24 EACH - VARIOUS SOUPS
FIVE CASES 24 EACH – 16 OUNCE POWDERED ENRICHED MILK
FIVE CASES 24 EACH – UNSALTED CRACKERS
FIVE CASES 24 EACH – 4 POUND BLOCK CHEESE
FIVE CASES 24 EACH - VARIOUS SWEETENED, DIETETIC COOKIES
FIVE CASES 24 EACH – POWDERED ENRICHED EGGS
FIVE CASES 24 EACH – 16 OUNCE POWDERED ENRICHED CITRUS JUICE
FIVE CASES 24 EACH – 16 OUNCE APPLE JUICE
FIFTY CASES 24 EACH – 24 OUNCE DISTILLED DRINKING WATER
FIVE CASES 24 EACH – 14 OUNCE ENRICHED

FARINA

CIVIL DISOBEDIENCE LEVEL = 0. THE HOLDER OF THIS ORDER MAY SELECT AN ADDITIONAL FIVE CASES OF THEIR CHOOSING.

"I have never seen a civil disobedience level of zero," the agent said. "They are usually a five or six. The higher the civil disobedience level, the less food is authorized."

The manager looked puzzled. "Who authorized this order?"

"A government healthcare agent named Joseph Victorio," the agent answered. He handed the manager an identification card. "It is a legitimate order. I checked the government population database." He looked toward the door. "The people who came to get it are all young, under the age of twenty."

"This is a lot of food," the manager said. "How are they going to carry it?"

"They are driving a white van," the agent answered.

The manager stood from his desk and walked to the door. He walked toward the rear of the food dispensing warehouse to the delivery area. Parked near the door was a white van. "Harvesters? Why are harvesters here?" The manager had a look of fear on his face. He was fifty-seven years old and he was afraid the harvesters had come for him.

"That is not a harvester's van," the agent answered. "The young people who came to pickup the order are driving it."

The manager frowned. He had a look of fear on his face. "That is a harvester's van. What are harvesters doing here?"

"That is not a harvester's van," the agent answered again. "The vans the harvesters use have seats in the rear and a section for their collection equipment. That van does not have any seats in the rear. There is nothing in the rear. It is just a white van."

The manager looked puzzled. He walked to his office as the agent followed him. He entered his office and accessed the government population database. He entered the name and identification number from the person's card. The system paused slightly. Then, the person's photograph and name appeared on his terminal screen. The photograph and name matched. He entered the section for food dispensing orders. He entered the order number. The system paused slightly. Then, the food order appeared on his terminal screen. The order matched.

"What is wrong with the system?" the manager asked. "It's slow!"

"I do not know," the agent answered. "It was fast this morning. I filled more than one hundred orders. When I entered the names and identifications numbers, the response was instantaneous." He pointed towards the order. "The system paused when I entered that information. It is like the system can not find it, then it looks elsewhere for the information. It's a legitimate order; some equipment malfunction?"

The manager leaned backwards in his chair, thinking. He reached for the communicator on his desk when the agent stopped him. "I would not do that!"

"Why?" the manager asked. "I think we should contact Mr. Victorio and verify this food order."

"It is against government law to question a healthcare agent's decision," the agent said. He looked worried. "The penalty for questioning a healthcare agent's decision is four years in prison." He looked toward the door. "I think it is a trick."

"Trick?" the manager asked.

"Trick," the agent answered. "It has happened before. Mr. Speaker will send people to a food dispensing warehouse with false orders. One manager questioned an order and contacted the healthcare agent. The agent was furious that his decision was questioned. The healthcare agent demanded to know who the manager was and where they were located."

"What happened?" the manager asked. He had a worried look on his face.

"Within thirty minutes, Soldiers of the Senate arrived at his location," the agent answered. "The manager was stunned! When he awoke, he was in a prison. No one ever saw him or heard of him again. I think he died in prison for disobeying Mr. Speaker's direct order not to question a healthcare agent's decision."

The manager looked worried. "Do we have enough food to fill the order?"

The agent laughed. He pointed towards the food order. "We have enough food to fill more than one thousand of those orders."

"No we don't," the manager said. "There is a food shortage. Several states are rationing food."

The agent laughed. "There is no food shortage. We have lots of food."

The manager looked puzzled. "Mr. Speaker announced that there is a food shortage."

The agent leaned forward towards the manager's desk. "I do not question anything Mr. Speaker says. He is our supreme leader. If he was here, I would bow at his feet and kiss his foot for the opportunity to serve him. If I didn't, I would be stunned by the Soldiers of the Senate and left to die where I stand." He rose upwards. "Mr. Joseph Victorio is a government healthcare agent. We must follow Mr. Victorio's decision and fill that order."

The manager nodded his head.

The agent smiled slightly. "When we finish that order, Mr. Victorio authorized twenty more just like it."

The manager rose from his seat. *Is it possible, a rogue healthcare agent who has enough courage to defy Mr. Speaker?* He walked to the reception area. In the area were young men and women. They all looked under the age of twenty. Several of the people held food orders in their hands. The manager walked to the front door. Parked outside the warehouse were more than twenty white vans. Several of the vans appeared to be damaged; there were small holes in the sides. *Bullet holes? It can't be. There are no guns!* As he looked outward, he could see several white vans approaching the parking area. These vans also looked damaged. Several of the vans had numerous small holes in the sides and one van did not have a windshield. Young people, men and women under the age of twenty, were driving the vans.

The manager laughed loudly.

He turned towards the young people standing in the reception area. "It will take a few minutes to load your vans. Please be patient. Some of these cases are heavy and we will need to verify each order. If your government healthcare agent is Mr. Joseph Victorio, I do not think there will be any problems." He motioned toward the agent. "Open some cans of fruit juice for these fine people."

The agent smiled and walked towards the warehouse area.

The manager walked to the reception counter. "Next order please?"

A young man and woman approached the counter and handed the manager their identification cards and the food order. The manager accessed the government population database. He entered the identification numbers and names. The system paused slightly. Then, the photographs and names appeared on the terminal screen. They matched. He entered the section for food dispensing orders. He entered the order number. The system paused slightly. Then, the food order appeared on his terminal screen. The order matched. *What is wrong with the system? It's slow.* He looked at the food order. It was designed for the elderly and the government healthcare agent who authorized the food order was Mr. Hammond Burke, not Mr. Joseph Victorio. *Who is he? Are there two rogue healthcare agents?*

The manager looked confused. *The system can not find the information so it looks elsewhere? He* laughed loudly. *It can't be! Somebody has hacked the government population database! These two healthcare agents do not exist!* He laughed very loudly. *However, real or not, we must follow Mr. Speaker's direct order and not question a healthcare agent's decision.*

He smiled at the young woman standing at the counter. "How would you like the soup selection? I recommend the tomato. It is very tasty and nutritious. It will put meat on your bones."

The young woman smiled. "Mrs. Diaz likes tomato soup. Thank you for your recommendation."

The manager nodded and smiled. "You have a civil disobedience level of zero. A score of zero means you can select an additional five cases of your choosing. May I suggest you select fresh fruit! We have mangos and peaches."

"Thank you," the young man said. "We will accept your suggestion of the fresh fruit." He turned towards the young woman standing beside him. "Mr. Kuwanta likes mangos."

The manager leaned forward. "Tell Mr. Kuwanta if he crushes the mangos and mixes it with the powdered milk, it makes a delicious, nutritious flavored drink." He winked at the young man.

The manager wrote on the order and laughed. "It will take a few minutes to prepare your order. Next order please?"

Three young men approached the counter and handed the manager their identification cards and food order.

"Good morning!" the manager said cheerfully. "It is a beautiful day!"

"No it isn't," one of the three young men said. He pointed towards the door of the reception area. "It is cloudy outside and it may rain."

The manager smiled and laughed. He looked at the young people standing in the reception area and the many white vans parked outside. The parking area was designed for one hundred fifty vehicles. He watched as the parking spaces were being quickly filled with white vans. Many of the vans were damaged. One van had external and internal damage: no windshield, multiple small holes in the front and sides, fender wells and hood. The van moved slowly in the parking area and it was followed by large amounts of black smoke from the tailpipe. *Those are harvesters' vans and those holes were made by bullets!*

He smiled at the young man who had spoken. "I beg to differ. It is a very beautiful, wonderful day!"

The manager paused and looked outward towards the parking area. "Yes, it is a very beautiful, wonderful day," he said quietly to himself. *Guns! Someone has real guns, lots of guns! The harvesters are gone and Mr. Speaker and his Soldiers of the Senate are next!*

Speaker of the Senate

The Speaker of the Senate, Cecil Morris, watched the crowd through his binoculars. They had gathered early, before 7:00 A.M., and made their usual demands: more food, more medical care, more jobs, more living credit units, more medication.

"More, more, more," he said bored. "What happened to better? Better food, better medical care, better jobs." He watched through his binoculars as the Soldiers of the Senate approached the small group from behind, a sneak attack.

One of the members of the group was yelling their demands towards the Capitol. The speaker could not hear what he was yelling. He was far enough away. His office was located on the second floor of the Capitol. This group was small, less than one hundred.

He smiled as the soldiers attacked the rioters from behind. He laughed as the people; men, women and children screamed and attempted to run away. The soldiers grabbed the rioters and threw them to the ground. Two soldiers grabbed their legs as one soldier removed their shoes and struck the soles of their feet with a cudgel. "Bastinado!" A crowd technique he learned at one of the leadership conferences. The soldiers used the new shillelagh he ordered; cudgel's made from hardwood not plastic or metal.

The speaker ordered the soldiers not to use their stunners on the rioters. Children shaking from electric shock only created larger crowds. A lesson he learned two years ago.

Bored, he turned from the window and walked to the stack of papers on his desk. He looked at the large number of requests from various states. *Food, medicine, jobs. These people should be grateful for what they have.*

He sat in his chair and used his plasticized stamp to respond to the requests. "Denied! Denied! Denied!"

The speaker leaned backwards in his chair. Being the supreme ruler of the United States was a lonely job. He had held the position since the overthrow of the House and executive branches of government in the year 2024. The sudden disappearance of the president and members of the House and the new political party made it necessary for the Senate to temporarily take control of the government.

Their takeover was ruled as not constitutional by the nine members of the Supreme Court. To protect the people, it was necessary to bring all armed forces under the control of the Senate. That action, by the Senate, was also ruled as not constitutional by the nine members of the Supreme Court. That problem was solved quite easily, no Supreme Court. It was necessary for the Senate to abolish the Supreme Court. The two old men and seven old women gave no resistance when they were led from their chambers by Soldiers of the Senate.

Fear of the Senate and the Soldiers of the Senate kept everyone in line. Problems were dealt with quickly, efficiently and permanently.

The speaker laughed. Ruling was not difficult. Make promises you can not keep. Blame your failure on others.

Knock! Knock!

The speaker stood from his chair. "Enter."

The Sergeant at Arms entered the Office of the Speaker of the Senate. "Mr. Speaker. We have a delegation from the state of Kansas. They want to speak to you concerning food rationing."

"Where is Owen?"

"He has already spoken to them," the sergeant answered. "They did not like his response and they demand to speak to you."

The speaker laughed. "They are in no condition to demand anything. Tell Owen he was appointed to take care of those types of problems. If he can't do it, I will appoint someone else to do it." He paused. "I don't like people coming here with demands."

The sergeant nodded. He looked towards the window. "We may have a problem."

"What problem?" the speaker asked. He was bored and sat in his chair.

The sergeant had a concerned look on his face. "Our intelligence reports a large number of people approaching the Capitol."

"What people?"

"Old men and old women," the sergeant answered.

The speaker laughed. "You are afraid of old men and old women?"

The sergeant had a concerned look on his face. "No. However, our intelligence reports more than ten thousand old men and old women are approaching the Capitol."

He looked nervously towards the window. "They are approaching from every direction."

"Did you send the military to stop them?"

"I did," the sergeant answered. He turned slightly. "Commander Brice sent two hundred soldiers to intercept them. I think something happened!"

"What happened? Did you order the soldiers to use their stunners?"

"Yes," the sergeant answered.

The speaker held his hands outwards. "What?"

"I don't know," the sergeant answered. "Our reports suddenly stopped when the soldiers began to charge them." He looked towards the window. "That report was received more than one hour ago."

He walked to the window of the Capitol. From where he stood, he could see the streets. He could see First Street NW and First Street NE. To his right was Independence Avenue and to his left was Constitution Avenue. Directly in front of his view was First Capitol Street. He looked outwards, thinking. Slowly, he noticed something. *People? Where are the people?*

The streets surrounding the Capitol were empty!

The streets of Washington D.C. were normally busy at 9:00 A.M. but the streets were empty. A small group of rioters approached the Capitol earlier. The rioters were in the walkway to the First Street entrance to the East Front of the Capitol. He looked where they had stood, yelling and screaming. The area was clear. The soldiers had been ordered not to arrest them. The soldiers had been ordered to punish them for their civil disobedience. He looked at that area and it was clear.

There was a strange silence outside the Capitol. The silence made the sergeant began to feel uneasy.

He looked outward, beyond the streets in front of the Capitol. Far away, he could see something approaching.

It looked like a long, dark line. The line appeared to be more than one city block deep. The dark line stretched from his left to his right. He looked towards his far right. He could not see New Jersey Avenue clearly but the line extended to New Jersey Avenue. He looked towards his far left. He could not see clearly but the line extended to Delaware Avenue.

The line moved slowly, surely towards the Capitol. He watched as the long line approached First Street from Independence and Constitution Avenues. At First Street the line split. One section of the line turned east and west onto First Street as two sections continued onward onto Independence Avenue and Constitution Avenue. The line continued to move slowly forward, completely filling the streets, and then it stopped.

The sergeant expected the people to scream and yell their demands but there were none. The people did not move or speak; they stood looking towards the Office of the Speaker of the Senate. The silence of the many thousands of elderly people surrounding the Capitol unnerved him.

The silence was deafening. The only sound he could hear was Mr. Speaker sitting at his desk writing on paper with a pen. He could hear the sound of the pen moving on the paper. The speaker was unaware of the event that had occurred.

The unexpected silence from the people was frightening and terrifying. His heart began to beat rapidly as their silence gave him an eerie premonition of doom. He waited and watched from the window expecting something, anything, to happen.

It seemed like hours but it was only minutes when the strange silence surrounding the Capitol was broken. The sergeant heard unfamiliar noises. He heard sounds like the scraping of metal. From the Office of the Speaker of the Senate, located on the second floor of the Capitol, he could hear thousands of clicking sounds.

Whatever was to happen had begun.

He turned to the speaker. "Mr. Speaker. They're here!"

SOL

The Speaker of the Senate looked outward from the window of his office in the Capitol. "How many are out there?"

"Mr. Speaker, I have no idea," the Sergeant at Arms answered. "Commander Bradley estimated ten to twenty thousand. They keep coming."

"Demands?" the speaker asked.

"Only one," the sergeant answered. "They are here to reclaim the government on behalf of the people, all of the people."

"Sons of Liberty," the speaker laughed. He looked through his binoculars. Each person held a stick-type device. In the front of the stick-type device was a round drum. The round drum-like device was pointed towards the Capitol and letters were painted on the drum. "S O L. What does S O L mean?"

The initials for their group," the sergeant answered. "S O L means Sons of Liberty."

The speaker laughed. "I see old men and old women. Shouldn't the letters read OS & OD O L?"

"I have no idea," the sergeant answered. He had initially been afraid of the large group but the presence of the military calmed his fears. There were more than two thousand soldiers surrounding the Capitol. "It doesn't matter; we are prepared to send the military to disperse them."

Joseph Victorio walked in front of the large group of senior citizens who had surrounded the Capitol of the United

States of America. "Our goal is to save, not to destroy!" Joseph yelled. "Our goal is to reclaim what our forefathers fought for and died for!" He walked briskly. "We will not allow our government to dictate who will live and who will die!"

"Roll call!"

Several people moved forward from the line of people who surrounded the Capitol.

"SAAG Alabama!" a woman yelled.

"SAAG Texas!" a man yelled.

"SAAG Oklahoma!" a man yelled.

"SAAG California!" several people yelled in unison.

"SAAG from the Volunteer State of Tennessee!" a woman yelled.

Cheers erupted from the people in the crowd.

"One thousand seven hundred forty-two SAAG patriots from the great state of Vermont!" a man yelled.

Loud cheers erupted from the people in the crowd.

"SAAG New York!" a woman yelled.

"SAAG from the Buckeye State of Ohio!" a man yelled proudly.

Cheers erupted from the people in the crowd.

"SAAG Kansas!" a man yelled.

"We just got here!" a woman yelled. She was breathing heavily. A large group of people, old men and old women, held their Chicago pianos upward. The group of people breathed heavily, as if they had been running. "Four hundred SAAG patriots from the Island State of Hawaii!" she screamed.

Loud cheers, screams and whistles erupted from the people in the crowd.

"SAAG New Mexico!" a woman yelled.

The roll call was interrupted as many of the people began to move backwards. "Soldiers of the Senate!" several people in the crowd yelled.

A large number of men, dressed in uniform, began to form a line between the people and the Capitol. The soldiers were holding stunners in their hands and on command, in unison, squeezed them. Large flashes of light could be seen and the numbers of flashes were blinding.

The people in the crowd began to move backwards. "Don't break ranks!" Joseph yelled. "Those stunners can not hurt you! They are out of range!"

The people moved back into their positions and pointed their Chicago pianos towards the Capitol.

"We almost broke them," the speaker said laughing. "Have the military advance on them! Send one hundred … no … send five hundred."

The sergeant spoke into a communicator. "Mr. Speaker has ordered five hundred Soldiers of the Senate to advance on the Sons of Liberty. Show no mercy!"

The speaker laughed. "What is the range of our stunners?"

"Three feet," the sergeant answered.

"Where did they get their stunners?" the speaker asked.

"Made them their self, I guess," the sergeant answered. "They look old and Commander Bradley thinks their range is in inches not feet. He thinks those round drums are some type of old battery. He also thinks they hold less than a full-type charge." He turned toward the speaker. "Mr. Speaker, they don't have a chance!"

"How far are the Sons of Liberty?" the speaker asked.

"They are afraid to come too close," the sergeant answered laughing. "Commander Bradley estimates they are between one hundred fifty and two hundred yards away."

The speaker looked at his wrist watch. "It will take ten to fifteen minutes for the military to advance to their front lines. Order the soldiers to walk slowly at first and then charge them when they are within fifty yards. Squeeze the stunners every step of the way."

The sergeant spoke into his communicator. "Advance slowly and then charge them at a distance of fifty yards. Activate the stunners with each step."

The military commander was listening to his communicator. "Forward at a slow pace!" the military commander yelled. "Activate stunners on your left step! Charge at a distance of fifty yards! Show no mercy! Forward!"

The soldiers began to move forward. They marched in unison and with each step of their left foot, they activated their stunner.

Zing. Zing.

The flashes of light were bright, intense.

Joseph watched the long line of soldiers approach their front line, west of the Capitol. "I need four volunteers!"

The entire west line moved forward.

Joseph walked in front of the men and women. He selected three women and one man. The four people stepped forward.

"Play them a tune in the key of C on my command!" Joseph yelled. The four people pointed their Chicago pianos towards the advancing soldiers.

The speaker laughed. He was observing the battle with his binoculars. "Three old women and one old man against five hundred," he laughed. "They should break at any time." He watched the soldiers advance toward the four people. The four people did not move. They held their objects towards the advancing soldiers. He could see the letters S O L painted on the drums.

"Any minute," the speaker said.

The four people did not move. The soldiers continued their advance.

"Any minute," the speaker said. "They will break ranks any minute."

The four people did not break ranks and run. They held their objects toward the advancing soldiers.

"Any minute," the speaker said. "There is about one hundred yards between them."

Rat-tat-tat. Rat-tat-tat.

The advancing soldiers fell to the ground. Many of the soldiers jerked as if they were in some type of pain.

Two of the fallen soldiers stood and began to run towards the Capitol.

Rat-tat-tat.

The two soldiers fell to the ground.

The speaker's eyes were widely opened. "They have some type of long range stunner!" He looked at the fallen soldiers through his binoculars; they had large spots of red on their uniforms. The soldiers were not moving. "Send more soldiers!"

"Some type of red poison!" the commander yelled. "Those explosions are sending capsules of red poison! Riot shields!"

The soldiers picked up their riot shields. The shields protected them from crowds throwing sticks and stones. They held their shields forward.

The commander was listening to his communicator, waiting for orders from the speaker. "Send more soldiers!" the Sergeant at Arms screamed into his communicator. "Send one thousand! Full charge! Show no mercy!"

"Units Able and Baker assemble!" the commander yelled. The soldiers quickly formed a protective line between the people and the Capitol.

"Full charge!" the commander yelled.

The soldiers began to run, in unison, towards the people. They held their riot shields in front of them as they squeezed their stunner.

Zing. Zing.

The flashes of light were bright, intense.

"SAAG patriots from the great states of Texas, Montana, Nevada and Utah advance!" Joseph yelled.

Sections of the front line parted as more than five hundred people, men and women, stepped forward. They held their Chicago pianos towards the soldiers running towards them.

"Fire!" Joseph yelled.

Rat-tat-tat. Rat-tat-tat.

The guns blazed as flashes of light erupted from the barrels. Large holes appeared on the front of the riot shields. The steel-jacketed bullets ripped through the shields, shattering them as the advancing soldiers fell.

Rat-tat-tat. Rat-tat-tat.

The S.A.A.G. patriots fired their guns wild, erratic. Bullets struck trees, the ground, cement walls and the Capitol itself. Windows cracked in the Capitol and chunks of cement were torn from the columns. The noise stopped in short bursts as the Chicago pianos had run out of ammunition.

"SAAG patriots from the great state of California advance!" Joseph yelled.

More than seven hundred men and women stepped from the front lines as Joseph pointed towards the windows of the Office of the Speaker of the Senate.

"Fire!" Joseph yelled.

Their guns blazed as bullets struck the glass of the windows in the Office of the Speaker of the Senate.

Loud thuds could be heard from inside. The speaker ducked as the glass window in his office began to crack. He watched in amazement as spider web-like lines appeared on the outside as a hundred then a thousand armor-piercing bullets struck it. The bullet proof glass in the window held briefly, and then it shattered. Loud thuds could be heard on the far wall. He looked upwards and backwards, to see gapping holes in the wall and one wooden door in shambles.

Rat-tat-tat. Rat-tat-tat.

Bullets continued to strike the Capitol as the remaining soldiers ran, screaming into the protection of the Capitol.

The noise stopped in short bursts as the Chicago pianos had run out of ammunition.

"SAAG Patriots from the great states of Hawaii, Tennessee, Alabama, Georgia, Kentucky and Florida advance!" Joseph yelled.

The entire south line moved forward. When the south line moved forward, the north line began to move outwards, away from the Capitol.

"They broke ranks!" the sergeant yelled excited. "The north line has moved east and west, away from the Capitol."

Joseph watched the north line move east and west, away from the Capitol. When the north line had moved out of range, Joseph ordered the south line to fire.

Rat-tat-tat. Rat-tat-tat. Rat-tat-tat.

The south line fired their Chicago pianos. Bullets struck the Capitol striking the walls, cracking then shattering windows, punctured doors and blew chunks of cement from the columns. One column cracked and partially fell. The seniors in the crowd cheered when bullets struck the flag pole atop the Capitol and the flag, which displayed the seal of the United States Senate, crashed to the roof.

Rat-tat-tat. Rat-tat-tat.

The guns blazed as one column, at the front entrance, cracked and fell to the ground. Slowly, one section of the dome partially collapsed inward.

The noise stopped in short bursts as the Chicago pianos ran out of ammunition.

"Reload!" Joseph yelled.

The patriots pressed a lever on their guns and the round drum dropped to the ground. They replaced the drum. The replaced drum had the letters S O L painted on the front.

"Hold!" Joseph yelled.

The Capitol was dark. More than fifty thousand steel-jacketed bullets fired from the south line struck the Capitol, damaging electrical circuits. The once brightly lit Capitol was plunged into darkness.

The patriots cheered when they saw multiple white flags being waved from the shattered windows and damaged doors.

Elections

The Speaker of the Senate walked slowly out of the front door of the Capitol. He was alone and waving a white piece of cloth. Joseph walked towards him, flanked by six S.A.A.G. patriots. The six seniors held their Chicago pianos towards the speaker. Hammond Burke was one of the six.

They met half way, between the front lines of the S.A.A.G. patriots and the damaged Capitol. "It's all yours," the speaker said, as he handed his gavel to Joseph.

Joseph looked at the object the speaker handed him. It was cylindrical, hourglass in shape and there was no handle. The object had a yellowish appearance and appeared to be made from the tusk of an animal. *Ivory?*

"It's real," the speaker said. "The gavel was a gift from the Republic of India in the year 1954. It's yours!"

Joseph looked puzzled. "I don't want your job."

The Speaker of the Senate looked puzzled. "What do you want?"

"Freedom," Joseph answered. "All we want is freedom."

The speaker looked puzzled. "You can have your freedom. I will abolish the Department of Harvesting."

"Not freedom for us," Joseph said. "We want freedom for everyone! We want elections. We want our leaders elected, by the people, not appointed."

"Elections?" the speaker asked puzzled.

Joseph reached into his coat pocket and he removed sheets of paper. "The Constitution of the United States as enacted in the year 1776."

The speaker took the papers and he looked at them curiously. "A copy of this was once displayed on the walls of the Senate Chambers." He began to read it and he laughed.

"You expect us to do this?" He laughed as he handed the papers to Joseph.

Joseph took the papers. "No," he answered. "We do not expect you to do anything. We are going to do it! We will begin meetings to elect our representatives based on the Constitution. When our leaders are elected, we are placing them in power."

The speaker looked puzzled. "How are you going to do that?"

"Force!" Joseph answered. "We are going to use force. When the people, all the people, have had an opportunity to vote, the Sons of Liberty are bringing our elected representatives to Washington and place them in power."

"Who are these elected representatives?" the speaker asked.

"I have no idea," Joseph answered. "That decision belongs to the people of the United States not the United States Senate."

Joseph dropped the speaker's gavel to the ground and carefully folded the Constitution of the United States. He placed the Constitution in his coat pocket.

Joseph looked to his left and right and he held his right hand upwards.

The people surrounding the Capitol began to slowly move backwards.

"Leaving? You are leaving?" the speaker asked puzzled.

Joseph nodded his head. "You have our demands."

"What was this all about?" the speaker asked. He pointed towards the damaged Capitol and the many people standing, surrounding the Capitol. The people were moving slowly backwards.

"A warning," Joseph answered. "This is a warning!"

The speaker pointed towards the Chicago pianos the six members of S.A.A.G. were holding. "Where did you get those stunners? We will purchase everyone you have!"

"They are not for sale. They are not stunners," Joseph said.

The speaker looked puzzled. He looked to his left and right at the soldiers who lay on the ground. "They are stunned!"

"They are not stunned." Joseph said. "They are harvested, dead!"

The speaker had a worried look on his face. "What are those things?"

"Choppers," Hammond Burke answered. "Trench sweeper, annihilator, Chicago typewriter, Chicago piano." Hammond paused. "Thompson submachine guns."

"There are no guns!" the speaker yelled. "All legal guns were confiscated in the year 2020. Those are not guns, they are stunners."

"Mr. Speaker, you are correct," Joseph said. "In the year 2020 all registered guns were confiscated and destroyed." He looked at the many people standing, holding guns. "It seems you missed a few. These guns are not legal, they are illegal."

"Where did you get them?" the speaker asked. His voice began to shake. "How many do you have?"

"We don't know for sure," Joseph answered. "We have not had time to recover all of the caches hidden in Arizona, Washington State, Alaska and Hawaii."

The speaker laughed. He laughed very loudly. "It doesn't matter! We have guns, we have lots of guns. They are hidden."

"Not anymore," Joseph said. "We found them! All you have is stunners."

The speaker laughed. "We have soldiers."

"Where are they?" Joseph asked. "I don't see any." He looked at the soldiers who lay on the ground. "The only ones I can see; can't help you."

"It doesn't matter," the speaker laughed. "The people of the United States will not allow this to happen." The Speaker of the Senate laughed. "Do you really think you can elect people and place them in power?"

"Yes," Joseph answered. "We will elect people and place them in power."

The speaker had a worried look on his face. "I don't think so," he said slowly. "It would take ten times the number of people here to do that."

Joseph smiled as he turned and walked away. He walked ten steps and turned. "We have more than enough! We didn't bring everybody."

"It doesn't matter how many you are! You are old and useless!" the speaker yelled.

"Not anymore," Joseph said slowly. "We proved that today."

The speaker shook his right fist at Joseph. "We will hunt you down like rabid dogs!"

"We are not difficult to find," Joseph said slowly.

"You are not patriots! You are revolutionaries! This is not liberty! This is tyranny!" the speaker yelled.

"Depends on what side you are on," Joseph said slowly. He turned and began walking away, towards the front lines.

"I am the most powerful person in the United States!" the speaker yelled. "I will not give up my power!"

"That decision is no longer yours to make," Joseph said.

"I will get you, your wives, your husbands and your children!" the speaker yelled.

Joseph winced. He stopped walking and turned toward the speaker. "What did you say?"

"I found your weakness!" the speaker laughed. "Children! We will enact a new law. All children under the age of five are to be harvested!"

"I don't think so," Joseph said angered. "I, we, would never allow that to happen."

"You are old and useless!" the speaker yelled. "I will get you, your wives, your husbands and your children! I have the power to do it!"

The speaker turned towards the people surrounding the Capitol. "My name is Cecil Morris! I am the Speaker of the United States Senate!" he yelled. "I am the most powerful person in the United States! I order you to disperse! I order you to drop your stunners and return to your homes! If you do not obey my orders, I will enact the Children's Harvesting Act of 2042! All children under the age of five will be harvested!"

The north, south, east and west lines were slowly moving backwards. When they heard the speaker yell, they stopped moving backwards and began to move forward. Thousands of clicking sounds could be heard.

Joseph raised his left hand and the lines stopped their advance and took an offensive position.

"How old are you?" Joseph asked. His eyes were widely opened and expressed anger, much anger.

"Sixty-seven!" the speaker yelled. "What difference does it make?" He turned towards the people surrounding the Capitol. "You have five minutes to drop your stunners and disperse!"

Joseph reached behind his back and he removed a pistol hidden underneath his coat. He pointed the pistol towards the speaker with two hands. ".44 magnum."

The speaker laughed. "You can't harvest me! I found your weakness, children and law. You love children and you claim to honor law!"

"We honor law when it suits us!" Joseph said. "Sections 501 and 505 of the Harvesting Act of 2032. All persons who have attained the legal age of sixty-five years are to be harvested."

"You can't harvest me!" the speaker yelled. "Politicians are exempt!"

"Mr. Speaker," Joseph said smiling. "You can't remember correctly." He pointed the gun he was holding towards the ground, where the speaker's gavel lay.

The speaker looked at his gavel lying on the ground. "So," he said. "What does that mean?"

"Mr. Speaker, you surrendered and you resigned," Joseph answered. "In resigning, you lost your exemption."

The speaker looked at Joseph. His eyes were widely opened as he looked at the gun in Joseph's hand. His eyes slowly narrowed. *That is not a gun. It's a stunner.* He was not afraid of a stunner! He would be stunned and taken to a medical clinic. The speaker would be given the best medical care, not like the others. In a few days he would be fine. In a few days, he would order the harvesting of everyone involved.

He expected Joseph to move but he did not move.

The speaker looked at Joseph with a snarl. He was waiting! *Go ahead. Do it if you have the nerve!*

Joseph paused. He appeared calm, but there was sadness in his eyes. His face slowly saddened. There appeared regret, remorse in his face for what he had almost done. *No.* He lowered the gun.

"You can't do it!" the speaker yelled. He laughed. His laugh was wild and maniacal. "You can't do it! I am to be harvested by my own law but you can't do it!"

"I can!" a voice came from the right.

The speaker looked to his right. His eyes widened and he began to move backwards. The person who spoke was approaching him. The person was reminiscent of photographs in old books he had seen. The photographs were of the cowboy. The cowboy carried hand guns in pouches attached to their waist and they carried additional ammunition on leather belts. The person approaching him was wearing a pouch attached to a belt tied at their waist. As the person walked towards him, their right hand reached to the pouch and pulled a shiny silver object from it. The person approaching him was not holding a stunner. In the person's right hand they were holding a gun, a big gun! In the old photographs, the sheriff killed the robber and the robber's body was displayed. The robber's body was filled with large holes.

The person approaching him was going to shoot him. He was going to be harvested, killed!

"No! No!" he pleaded. His eyes and face showed great fear. He looked at the soldiers lying on the ground with red on their uniforms. They were dead not stunned. They were shot by real guns.

He looked at the large numbers of people who surrounded the Capitol. They held guns, real guns. He moved backwards as the person who had spoken approached him.

"I order you to stop! I Am the Speaker of the Senate!"

The person continued walking towards him. Their eyes were cold, deadly! The person pointed the gun towards him.

He moved backwards. "I order you to stop! I Am the Supreme Ruler of the United States!"

The person walking towards him did not stop. He saw one of their thumbs move on the gun and he heard a click sound.

"No! No!" He attempted to turn and run but he tripped on his feet and he fell onto the ground.

The person approaching him stopped walking. The person seemed to pause. The person was waiting. The silver colored gun was aimed at his back as he attempted to crawl towards the safety of the Capitol.

"No! No!" the speaker begged as he crawled towards the Capitol. He looked backwards in fear and stopped crawling when he saw the person approaching him had stopped walking towards him. *She can't do it either! Cowards!* He stood upright laughing and screamed to the people standing in the crowd. "I order you to disperse!"

The people surrounding the Capitol did not move.

The speaker snarled. He turned to the person pointing the gun towards him. "You want government? You already have a government! I Am the Government!"

"Not any more!"

Boom!

The bullet struck the speaker in his right lung and he was pushed backwards, more than seven feet.

Boom!

The second bullet struck his left lung and he was thrown backwards and fell to the ground.

Catherine Meadows was standing less than twenty feet from the speaker. On her waist she wore a leather gun belt and across her chest, two leather belts filled with cartridges. She held the .357 stainless steel magnum in both hands and the force of the two rounds jerked the gun upwards, above her head.

"That is for my father! If my father and his friends were here, they would have stopped you ten years ago."

She lowered the gun and placed it in the holster. Catherine walked to Joseph and placed her right hand on his shoulder.

"I could not do it," Joseph said sadly. "I wanted to, but I could not kill a man in cold blood."

"Use them without regret and use them without remorse," Catherine said. "If the events were reversed, he would not have hesitated. That is the difference in you and him. He has no conscious and you do. He didn't care about anyone but himself. You risked your life to protect the aged."

Catherine looked at the many people standing, surrounding the Capitol, and the Capitol in ruins. "I had the advantage. My father and his friends were not crazy, they knew this would happen fifty-six years ago and they prepared me. What is left of the government is afraid, very afraid!"

"When the Government fears the people, there is liberty," Joseph said.

Catherine nodded her head, no, as she removed her hand from his shoulder. "It's not over yet! This is just a small battle. My father and his friends told me they will not give up their power easily. There is no liberty, yet! We will have to battle them in every city and every state." She paused, thinking. "My father told me what to do!" *Guns alone do not win wars. You need the people, all of the people!*

She turned towards the people standing, surrounding the Capitol. "No one is free until everyone is free!" she screamed. "All Americans must put aside their differences and stand together as one!"

The people in the crowd cheered.

She began to walk towards the front line. As she walked, she removed her father's gun from his holster and raised it into the air. "The Second American Revolution has begun!"

Loud cheers erupted from the people in the crowd.

"Liberty and Freedom for all! Stand together as one!" she began to chant, as she walked in widening circles and held her father's gun in the air.

The people in the crowd screamed and cheered.

"Liberty and Freedom for all! Stand together as one!" the people in the crowd began to chant.

Nevada Campaign

The twelve white vans moved slowly on the dark street. The twelve vans were flanked by military soldiers. The soldiers walked slowly and surrounded the vans. In their hands, they held stunners. The small convoy moved slowly on the deserted street towards the city hospital.

"How many?" one of the six harvesters in the first van asked.

"It doesn't matter," one of the six harvesters answered. "We are to harvest everyone lying in their beds. It is a show of force ordered by the new Speaker of the Senate."

"Everyone?" one of the harvesters asked puzzled.

"Everyone," one of the six harvesters answered. "It doesn't matter if they are young or old. It doesn't matter if they are women or children. Everyone!"

The small convoy moved slowly as the soldiers appeared nervous. They looked to their left and right. The entire city of Las Vegas was dark.

"Where are the lights?" one of the six harvesters asked. He looked outward to see darkness.

"Turned off," one of the six harvesters answered. "The new speaker ordered the entire power of the city cut. That includes the hospital. All emergency devices in the hospital have been deactivated. Use your electronic lanterns."

The small convoy moved slowly on the street and turned left where a barricade was set up to block the street. On the barricade was a series of lights. The lights looked old and the light was a small flame that came from a burning piece of cloth.

"Move it!" the commander of the soldiers ordered.

Three soldiers walked nervously towards the barricade and the lights. Attached to the barricade was a sign.

WARNING: THIS AREA IS UNDER THE PROTECTION OF S.A.A.G. UNAUTHORIZED PEOPLE AND VEHICLES WILL BE MET WITH DEADLY FORCE!

THE SONS OF LIBERTY

The soldiers looked puzzled. Far down the street, they could see the hospital. There were lights!

"I thought all the lights were turned off?" one of the three soldiers asked.

"Move the barrier!" the commander yelled.

The soldiers moved the barricade from the street entrance to the sidewalk and the small convoy began to move slowly towards the hospital.

As they approached the hospital, they saw something in the street. The convoy stopped! The van lights were set to bright. Standing in the street, in front of the hospital, were several old men and women. In their hands, they held some type of stunner. There was a round device on the front of their stunners and there were letters on the device – S O L.

The soldiers moved in front of the vans and activated their stunners.

Zing. Zing.

The flashes from their stunners were bright, intense. The old people standing in front of them began to move their heads to protect their eyes from the bright headlights of the van and the bright flash of the soldier's stunners. The surrounding darkness behind them and the bright lights in front of them hurt their eyes. They kept moving their heads to the left and right to protect their eyes.

"They can't see!" the commander laughed. "Some protection?"

Voom!

Suddenly, large lights were turned on behind the people standing in front of them. The large lights were placed to the left and right, above the people, standing in front of the hospital. The lights blazed and washed out the light from the headlights of the vans and the flashes from the stunners.

In the light of the large lamps, the soldiers could see additional old men and women standing towards their left on the sidewalk. They also held some type of stunner.

Voom!

Suddenly, large lights were turned on behind the people standing on the sidewalk. The convoy was bathed in a bright, intense white light that came from in front of them and to their left side. The large bright lights blinded the commander and the soldiers. They held their left hand upwards to protect their eyes.

"Old men and old women!" the commander yelled. "Charge!"

Zing. Zing.

Rat-tat-tat. Rat-tat-tat.

Boom! Boom!

Rat-tat-tat.

Alabama Campaign

The voting line was extremely long. The line began at the entrance to the voting tent. The tent was constructed in a vacant lot on Decatur Street, southeast of Moulton Heights in downtown Decatur, Alabama. The vacant lot was, at one time, a store where food could be purchased. The building was demolished and a statue of the new Speaker of the Senate was scheduled to be erected in its place. The line stretched from the tent entrance to a full one-mile in length.

"Who do you like?" one potential female voter asked a man standing in line behind her.

"They are all good," the man answered. "I have only heard two speak, but I liked what I heard. They both demand free elections and a repeal of all laws enacted against free speech."

The woman looked at her ballot. "I never thought voting would be so difficult. Every candidate is good!"

The man looked at her sample ballot, it contained many names. "You have the old ballot, I have the new ballot."

She looked at his ballot. The ballot he held had fewer names. Many of the names on her ballot had been removed. "What happened?"

The man laughed. "Many of the candidates realized if their names remained on the ballot, there may be a runoff election. All of the candidates met and they decided amongst themselves who was the better qualified. Many candidates withdrew their names so the process could move more swiftly."

"Amazing!" the woman said. "Patriots who care enough about their country to step aside for someone who is more qualified."

The people stood in line waiting to vote as a small convoy of military vehicles moved north along Bee Line Highway to 8th Avenue SE. The convoy was composed of military transports. The convoy moved slowly and stopped within fifty yards of the opening to the voting tent.

Government soldiers quickly exited the transports and stood in formation. Each soldier held a stunner.

The commander exited the last vehicle in the line and walked towards the front. In his hand he held an electronic speaking device. "You are violating government law by voting!" he yelled into the device. "You are ordered to disperse and return to your living units!"

The people standing in line to vote turned towards the commander and soldiers. There appeared to be more than one hundred soldiers with stunners. The people did not move.

"Do not be afraid!" the commander yelled into the device. He held upward a small card. "Mr. Speaker has ordered that all citizens who show loyalty to him will receive this card. This card authorizes additional living credits. This card guarantees you special treatment at any government health clinic. You will not have to stand in line."

The people standing in line to vote did not move or speak.

"Free food and additional medical care!" the commander yelled into the device. "Do not be afraid. Come to where we are standing and we will protect you! We will give you the card. Then, you must return to your living units!"

The people standing in line to vote did not move or speak.

The commander was irritated. "If you do not disperse, we are ordered to use force! It is against the government to vote! You are breaking the law and risking prison!"

The people standing in line to vote did not move or speak.

One of the soldiers moved to stand beside the commander. "What is wrong with these people?"

"Fear," the commander answered. "They are afraid of Mr. Speaker." He held upwards the speaking device. "It is against government law to vote! Your representatives are appointed not elected! If you have a problem, contact your appointed representative! They will contact you within six to eight months!"

The people standing in line to vote did not move or speak.

"We are authorized to use force!" the commander yelled. "If you do not immediately disperse, the new Speaker of the Senate has authorized us to use our stunners at full power! The charge will fry your eyeballs and explode your liver! We will leave you on the streets of Decatur to die in pain! You will not be taken to a medical clinic!"

Several of the people standing in line moved sideward as two people emerged from the voting tent. The two people were elderly and they both held Chicago pianos. The two people moved to stand in front of the line of people and they pointed their Chicago pianos upwards.

"We are not afraid of you!" the commander yelled into the speaking device. "We have one hundred fifty armed soldiers. They have stunners and we have been authorized to use them!"

The two people did not move. They held their Chicago pianos upwards.

"We are authorized to set our stunners on high!" the commander yelled into the speaking device. "The charge will fry your eyeballs and explode your liver! We will leave you to die on the streets of Decatur!"

The two people moved into a defensive position.

The commander looked worried. He had expected the people to run but they did not. He had expected many people to accept the new speaker's generous offer of additional food and expedited medical care, but no one accepted.

"Positions!" he yelled to the soldiers.

The soldiers quickly grouped into a single line of twenty five, six lines deep. They held their stunners upwards and squeezed them.

Zing. Zing.

Flashes of light leapt from the ends extending a distance of three feet. The flashes of light were bright, intense.

The people standing in line to vote did not move or speak. They looked towards the two people standing in front of them. The two people, members of S.A.A.G., were positioned to protect them.

"This is your last warning!" the commander yelled into the speaking device. "You are breaking government law by voting! You do not vote for your representatives! Your representatives are appointed! If you do not disperse immediately, we are authorized to use force! We will set our stunners on medium. The charge will fry your eyeballs! We will allow you to lie on the street and suffer and then we will set our stunners on high! The charge will explode your liver and your brain! Your brain will be splattered on the streets of Decatur!"

The two people holding Chicago pianos stepped forward.

The commander laughed. "You people are crazy!" he yelled into the speaking device. "You will die for the chance to vote? You are ungrateful! The government has given you everything! The government has given you food, clothing, shelter and medical care! What more do you want?"

The commander was angered. "The Speaker of the Senate is your supreme leader! You should bow at his feet and kiss his foot for the opportunity to serve him!"

The two people holding Chicago pianos stepped forward as the people standing in line frowned. They looked at each other with angry looks on their faces.

"The speaker has been generous, magnanimous!" the commander yelled into the speaking device. "We will show no mercy! Your brains will cover the street where you stand! We will take the names from the voting boxes and imprison every person who has voted!"

The two people, members of S.A.A.G., stepped forward two paces. They had angry looks on their faces and they pointed their Chicago pianos upwards. They slowly lowered them towards the soldiers and the commander. The letters S O L could be seen on a round drum located at the front. The commander, the soldiers, and the people standing in line to vote could hear two clicking noises.

The commander looked towards his left. "What are they holding?"

"Stunners," the soldier answered. "According to our intelligence, their stunners are hand made and have a range of one foot. They hold a charge less than our lowest setting."

"What does S O L mean?" the commander asked.

"Sons of Liberty," the soldier answered. "The letters S O L is for Sons of Liberty."

The commander looked worried. The two elderly men standing in front of him were not speaking. None of the people standing in line to vote were speaking. Everyone was silent. Their silence unnerved him. He expected the people to scream and yell, but they did not. The commander had encountered many people engaged in the actions of civil disobedience over the years but he had never encountered rioters who were silent.

He had heard of the Sons of Liberty. In the battle of Washington, they attacked the Capitol. In the battle, the Speaker of the Senate lost his life leading a charge to disperse them. According to rumor, the Sons of Liberty had a new type of stunner that damaged the Capitol.

The commander did not believe the rumor. When he was ordered to the Capitol, months after the battle, there was no damage. The Capitol was in the process of renovation. Mr. Speaker's office and living quarters was moved from the second floor to the fourth floor. Soldiers of the Senate were placed every twelve feet in the hallways and the many wooden doors were replaced by metal doors. Metal shutters were placed inside the Capitol before the new glass windows. He was told by the new Speaker of the Senate that all of the rioters had been harvested.

Who are these two people? Their silence was eerie and frightening. Their silence could only mean one thing; they had lost all fear of the government. If the people standing in line to vote had also lost all fear, the government has lost all control.

"They are not afraid. Has this happened before?"

"Many times," the soldier answered. "It is happening all over the state of Alabama. Soldiers have been sent to stop the elections and according to our reports, each election area was protected by two members of SAAG with stunners."

"Who is SAAG?" the commander asked.

"I have no idea," the soldier answered.

"What happened?" the commander asked. He looked at the two old men standing in front of the line of people waiting to vote. They held stunners. The two old men did not appear to be afraid.

"Success," the soldier answered. "Complete success."

The commander smiled. "The soldier's won?"

"Completely," the soldier answered. "We received a report of two members of S.A.A.G. protecting the place where people were voting. After the initial report, the reports stopped."

"Stopped?" the commander asked puzzled.

"Stopped," the soldier answered. "We received an initial report and no more reports. The mission was a success. If there had been problems we would have received a follow up report."

The commander laughed. He sounded a sound of relief. "Two against one hundred twenty-five and our stunners have a range of three feet. They are out-manned and out-stunned!" He laughed very loudly.

"You have been warned!" the commander yelled into the speaking device. He turned towards the soldiers. "We are fifty yards from them," he said quietly. "At twenty-five yards, break into a full run. Show no mercy." His voice lowered. "Harvest everybody standing in line! I want to see blood and guts. I want to see bodies and brains lying on the street."

He turned towards the voting tent and screamed into the electronic speaking device. "You have been warned! Forward!"

The soldiers began to move forward. They marched in step and activated their stunners with each step of their left foot.

Zing. Zing.

The flashes of light from the stunners were bright, intense. The soldiers marched forward five steps when a strange sound was heard.

Rat-tat-tat. Rat-tat-tat.

The World Turned Upside Down

The Speaker of the Senate looked bored as Commander Bradley began the briefing. "The only change is one group is continuing to move east and their numbers have increased."

"What group?" the speaker asked.

"The Sons of Liberty," Commander Bradley answered. He pointed towards a map of Washington D.C. "Our intelligence states that these four groups have not changed position. There are twenty to the east and west and twenty to the north and south. Their distance is approximately thirty miles from the Capitol. They have been there for five days."

"How many states are under the control of the Sons of Liberty?" the Sergeant at Arms asked.

Commander Bradley pointed towards the map. "This one, this one, this one, this one, this one, this one…"

The speaker raised his hand to stop the commander. "If what you say is correct, it appears we are surrounded. Let me rephrase the question. Which states are not under the control of the Sons of Liberty?"

"Our intelligence may not be accurate," Commander Bradley answered. "Only one."

"And?" the speaker asked. He was visibly irritated.

"Washington D.C.," the commander answered.

"However," the Sergeant at Arms said. "We are perfectly safe. The war has not gone well for us. We have new weapons."

"What new weapons?" the speaker asked.

"Stunners!" the commander answered proudly. "We have had our best minds working on the problem since this war began four years ago." He waved his hands in the air. "We held old technology. Our old stunners had a range of three feet and each system only held thirty charges. Our new stunners have a range of four feet and each unit holds sixty charges."

"Impressive," the speaker said. He stood slowly. "How many soldiers do we have?"

"Seven hundred," the commander answered. "They have been positioned around the city to protect the Capitol."

The speaker walked towards the map. The map was of the United States and each state had a black pin stuck into it. "What do these black pins mean?"

"The black pins indicate the Sons of Liberty have taken control of that state," the commander answered. "The white pin is us."

The speaker nodded his head. "Twenty, twenty, twenty, twenty," he said slowly. "That is eighty and we have seven hundred soldiers with the new stunner." He turned towards the commander. "Explain this group that is moving east?"

The commander smiled. He walked towards the map and pointed towards the Midwest. "They began to gather in the city of Topeka, Kansas five days ago."

"Their numbers?" the speaker asked.

"Fifty," the commander answered. "According to our intelligence reports, this was the last state to hold elections. They began to gather in this location when the election results were certified."

The speaker looked thoughtful. "Fifty plus eighty is one hundred thirty. We have seven hundred soldiers. Continue!"

"Strange," the commander said. "I do not understand their battle tactics. We fully expected them to return to Washington D.C. but they did not." He pointed towards the map. "We pulled every soldier from every city and every state, to protect the Capitol. We were waiting for them to return but they did not return. While our troops were stationed here, they began to take control of various cities and states." He turned to look at the speaker. "They held elections for the position of governor, and then went to another state."

"What is a governor?" the speaker asked.

The commander shrugged his shoulders. "Someone who is in control of that state," he answered.

"Strange," the speaker said. "Continue."

The commander smiled. "Our intelligence reported that more than five days ago, these governors met in Topeka, Kansas. An election was held and now one of the governors is the president."

"Was there an election for the Speaker of the Senate?" the speaker asked.

"Our intelligence does not report that," the commander answered.

"Strange," the speaker said. "Continue."

The commander smiled. "Five days ago, our intelligence reported that a large group of people, including the governors and the president, began moving east."

"How many?" the speaker asked.

"Fifty," the commander answered.

The speaker looked thoughtful. "One hundred thirty plus fifty is one hundred eighty. We have seven hundred. Continue."

The commander pointed towards the map. "They began to move east and somewhere towards the edge of Kansas, several smaller groups joined them."

"How many?" the speaker asked.

"Not sure," the commander answered. "The estimated total number is two hundred fifty."

"Two hundred fifty minus fifty is two hundred," the speaker said. "One hundred eighty plus two hundred is three hundred eighty. We have seven hundred." He turned quickly towards the commander. "I don't like those odds!"

"We have the new stunners," the sergeant said.

"How many troops do we have?" the speaker asked.

"Seven hundred," the commander answered puzzled. "We have seven hundred and they have been positioned around the city."

"I seem to recall more troops than seven hundred," the speaker said.

"Four years ago, we had more than sixty thousand troops," the commander said.

"Where are they?" the speaker asked.

The commander pointed towards the map. "Four years ago, after the battle of Washington, all troops were ordered to the city. We had sixty thousand troops stationed in and around Washington."

The speaker looked puzzled. He walked to his chair and sat down. "If all of the troops were in Washington, who was protecting the cities and the states?"

"No one," the commander answered. "All troops were ordered to Washington to protect the city."

"That was a stupid order!" the speaker yelled. "Who gave that order?"

The commander looked puzzled. "You did. When you were appointed Speaker of the Senate, you became the supreme ruler of the United States. You ordered all troops brought to the city to protect you."

"O yes," the speaker said slowly. "What else did I do?"

"You ordered troops to the states when the Sons of Liberty began to take control of them," the sergeant answered.

"Where are they?" the speaker asked.

"Deserted," the commander answered sadly. "Every troop we sent to reclaim those cities and states deserted."

"How do you know that?" the speaker asked.

"Obvious," the commander answered. "They never returned."

Force Majeure

"Where are they going?" the speaker asked. He held his hands outwards. "What is east of Kansas?"

"I have no idea," the commander answered. "All we know is there was some sort of election and everyone is moving east. They began to move east five days ago and that is when the groups of people began to appear near the city. We expected them to enter the city but they did not. They appear to be waiting for something."

The speaker looked puzzled. "Five days, five days. How far away from Washington D. C. is Topeka, Kansas?"

"One thousand one miles or one thousand six hundred eleven kilometers, as the crow flies," the commander answered. "I do not think they are coming here. If they were, they would have to travel a minimum of two hundred miles a day. They would be here in a matter of hours not days." He shrugged his shoulders. "They are not coming here."

"One thousand miles is a long distance for two hundred fifty. How are they traveling?" the speaker asked.

"Some type of military-type transport," the commander answered.

"What type of transport?" the sergeant asked.

"Not sure," the commander answered. "They look like the type of transport the military uses but the ones they have are old and damaged."

"Damaged?" the speaker asked.

"Damaged," the commander answered. "According to our intelligence, their climate condition systems are not working. June has been a very hot month. The last days of June have been very hot and small holes have been drilled into the sides, front and back of the transports. There are hundreds of small holes drilled into the transports to cool the people riding inside. They are not ours because ours are painted a camouflage green. These transports are painted with stripes of red, white and blue. Large white stars are painted on the blue stripes."

"Where are they now?" the speaker asked.

"Not sure," the commander answered. "We had more than twenty observers following them. They were placed strategically behind them. Yesterday, the reports suddenly stopped. We believe it is an equipment malfunction and we expect to begin receiving reports at anytime."

He pointed towards the map. "The last report was received at 09h00 CDT. That is 9:00 A.M. Central Daylight Time." The commander turned towards the speaker. "Their position was an estimated thirty-two miles northwest of Washington. They were last reported in Leesburg, Virginia. According to our last report, their numbers had increased dramatically. There were three hundred."

"Leesburg, Virginia?" the speaker asked puzzled. He held his hands outwards. "What is in Leesburg, Virginia?"

"I have no idea," the commander answered. He turned and pointed towards the map. "They began to gather in Leesburg, Virginia. Our intelligence reports three hundred are currently in Leesburg, Virginia. They have been there a minimum of two days."

The speaker looked worried. "Eighty plus three hundred is three hundred eighty. We have seven hundred troops."

The sergeant smiled. "More than enough. We have seven hundred troops and they have three hundred eighty. We have almost twice their number."

"I am sorry, I did not hear what you said," the commander said.

The speaker leaned forward. "Basic math!" he said irritated. "Seven hundred divided by three hundred eighty gives 1.82. We have almost twice the number of troops they have."

"No," the commander said puzzled. "Three hundred eighty thousand divided by seven hundred is five hundred forty-two." He pointed towards the map. "There are eighty thousand Sons of Liberty positioned thirty miles to the north, south, east and west of the city of Washington and three hundred thousand Sons of Liberty positioned thirty-two miles northwest of the city of Washington in the city of Leesburg, Virginia."

He paused. "We only have seven hundred troops."

The speaker frowned. "Where are the harvesters?"

The commander and the sergeant looked at each other with angry looks.

"Where are the harvesters?" the speaker asked again.

"Gone," the commander answered. "I made numerous requests to place the harvesters under the command of the military but my requests were denied."

"No reason to transfer command," the sergeant said. He turned toward the speaker. "They began to desert before the battle of Washington."

"They did not desert," the commander said. "They were eliminated."

The sergeant stood and yelled. "You have no proof!"

"Where are they?" the commander yelled. "That is your proof!"

The sergeant looked towards the speaker. "They began to disappear in the weeks and months prior to the battle of Washington."

"Weeks and months," the commander laughed. "The harvesters disappeared in a matter of days." He looked towards the speaker. "They began to disappear after the government population database was discovered to be compromised."

"You have no proof!" the sergeant yelled. "It was an equipment malfunction. The person who controlled the database deserted."

"We have four soldiers missing! Database controller missing! Damaged door? Wires cut?" the commander yelled. "Missing vans and human blood discovered in harvesting control rooms? No more harvesting! What more proof do you need?"

The speaker raised his hand and the commander and the sergeant stopped yelling at each other.

"How many harvesters did we have?" the speaker asked.

"Eighty-seven thousand four hundred sixteen," the sergeant answered.

The speaker's eyes widened.

"They were eliminated!" the commander yelled. He glared at the sergeant. "We do not know how or by who but eighty-seven thousand four hundred sixteen harvesters were eliminated in a matter of days not weeks or months. We have not had one report of harvesting since several weeks before the battle of Washington, four years ago. The Sergeant at Arms hired replacements but they were also eliminated."

The sergeant looked at the speaker. "If the commander is referring to that simple job in Las Vegas, his soldiers did not have the nerve to harvest everyone in that hospital. His soldiers deserted and forced my harvesters to go with them!"

"That is enough!" the speaker yelled as he shrugged his shoulders. "This is an old argument. The former speaker settled that argument. It was an equipment malfunction at the federal building and the harvesters deserted." He raised his hands. "As to Las Vegas, there were more soldiers than harvesters. It is obvious the soldiers deserted and they forced the harvesters to go with them. Those matters are closed and I do not want them discussed again. The matter before us is the Sons of Liberty."

The sergeant glared at the commander. He smiled as he sat in his chair. "Thank you Mr. Speaker for your support."

The speaker nodded as he looked at the map on the wall. "Here?" he asked puzzled. "They are coming here?"

"Perhaps," the commander answered. He was angered at Mr. Speaker's support of the sergeant and turned towards the wall. *They are coming here! And when they get here, the Sergeant at Arms is the first to go! If I play my cards carefully, I will be appointed the new Sergeant at Arms. Play the game and keep my aces hidden. I must show loyalty to the sergeant until his obvious end that is coming. Mr. Speaker will reward my loyalty and devotion in his new administration.* He smiled and turned towards the sergeant.

"I think the group has split," the sergeant said.

"Explain?" the speaker asked.

"It has happened before," the sergeant answered. "There is fighting among the groups and they split. It is possible the groups surrounding the city are here to protect us. They are loyal to their government and there will be a major battle when the two groups meet."

"What is your rationale?" the speaker asked.

"Obvious," the sergeant answered. "The group surrounding the city began to form when the final elections were held. They have not advanced into the city and they appear to be waiting. If they were to attack the city, they would already have done so."

"This group surrounding the city; are they causing problems?" the speaker asked.

"None," the commander answered slowly. "People are allowed to move freely into and out of the city. The only people who are not allowed to leave the city are politicians."

"Politicians?" the sergeant asked puzzled.

"Politicians," the commander answered. "Senator's Kane and Bradshaw attempted to leave the city but they were turned back."

"Were they harmed?" the speaker asked.

"No. Just turned back," the commander answered. "They were not allowed to leave the city." *Kiss up time! I will play the ace of clubs.* "The Sergeant at Arms may be correct! They were refused exit because the group could not protect them if they left the city." He nodded towards the sergeant. *I will repaint your blue office in the color of military green.*

"Possible," the speaker said. He looked puzzled. "You said they held their elections. How many elected officials do they have?"

"Not sure," the commander answered. "There is a governor from every state and one president, one vice president." He laughed. "They have more than one senator."

"What is funny about that?" the speaker asked. "We have twenty senators and one Speaker of the Senate. The only difference is that the senators are appointed."

"They have something called a congressman," the commander said. He smiled at the sergeant. *I am going to replace your desk and get a new one. Mr. Speaker will authorize it.*

"What are they?" the speaker asked.

"I do not know," the commander answered. "According to our intelligence reports, the number of senators and congressmen are based on some formula related to the population in each state. They have no way of knowing those numbers. They would need access to the government population database to know the numbers."

"Curious," the speaker said. "If the Sons of Liberty are coming here, to the city of Washington D.C., why would they bring their elected representatives with them? All positions of power are currently filled."

The Final Push Forward

Joseph Victorio stood in front of members of S.A.A.G. The large group was positioned thirty-two miles northwest from the nation's Capitol in the city of Leesburg, Virginia. He was standing on the roof of a military transport that had been taken in the Texas Campaign. The transport had been repainted in the colors of the flag of the United States of America. The hood was painted blue and large white stars were painted on the blue background.

"Today is Wednesday July 4, 2046!" he yelled. "We have come here today to reclaim our country in the name of the people; all of the people! We have come here today not to destroy our government; we have come here today to rebuild our government! We have not come here today as conquerors; we have come here today as liberators!"

The people in the large crowd screamed.

"Will the elected representatives of the people of the United States of America please raise your right hand?"

More than seven hundred right hands were raised in the crowd: president, vice president, senators, congressmen, congresswomen, governors and nine Supreme Court Justices.

The people in the large crowd screamed and cheered.

Joseph raised his hands and slowly, the screams and cheers stopped.

He looked at the large number of people standing in front of him. Joseph looked at the large number of right hands held upwards. "You have been elected by the people of the United States of America as their representatives and you are duly sworn to uphold the Constitution of the United States of America!" Joseph yelled.

The people in the large crowd were quiet.

"You have been elected by the people of the United States of America to represent the people, all of the people!" he yelled.

The people in the large crowd were quiet.

Joseph leaned forward towards the people holding their right hands upward. "We will not advance one foot, one inch, until you swear before God and country that you will protect the strong and the weak!" he screamed.

"We will not advance one foot, one inch, until you swear before God and country to protect every man, woman and child born, and in the womb yet to be born, within the boarders of the United States of America!" Joseph screamed.

"Do you so swear before God and country?"

"I do!"

The people in the large crowd screamed and cheered.

Joseph nodded as he stepped from the roof of the transport and walked to the rear. "Madam President. Madam Vice President. Will you please take your respective positions?"

The two women nodded. The transport was damaged in the Texas Campaign but it had been repaired to be as comfortable as possible. They stepped into the back of the transport. Six seats had been prepared to the sides and they sat in two of the seats. In the center of the transport was placed three metallic boxes. The boxes were made of titanium steel and hermetically sealed. A clear top revealed the documents preserved inside. One box contained an original signed Declaration of Independence. One box contained an original United States Constitution. One box contained an original Bill of Rights. The three documents were hidden in the year 1814 and preserved in the year 1986.

Four S.A.A.G. members entered the transport and sat in the remaining four seats. In their hands they held Chicago pianos. Large numbers of S.A.A.G. members quickly surrounded the vehicle.

Joseph closed the rear doors and he walked to the front of the transport. He looked to a large number of S.A.A.G. members who were positioned. They would march forward in front of the transport that would carry the elected president and vice president of the United States of America and the preserved charters of freedom.

"Are we ready?" Audrey laughed as she placed three leather pouches on Joseph's shoulders.

Joseph laughed at Audrey. She was holding a flintlock pistol in her right hand with three leather pouches across her chest.

"You can't go without this!" Catherine laughed as she handed Joseph a flintlock rifle. "It is a 1795 Springfield infantry musket."

He looked at the rifle. "Where did you get it?"

"Hidden in the original cache," Catherine answered. "The Sons of Liberty hid them during the War of 1812. They were hidden in the year 1814 when the British burned Washington."

"How many rifles were hidden?" Joseph asked puzzled.

"There are less than three hundred," Catherine answered. "There are two hundred seventy-nine rifles and eighty-seven pistols."

Joseph looked at the rifle. "It looks in good shape. Does it work?"

"It didn't in the year 1986," Catherine answered. "They were damaged by age and weather." She laughed. "My father and his friends repaired them. They improved them. Don't worry, it works. They all work!"

"Repaired?" Joseph asked. "Improved?"

"Replaced the wood stocks," Catherine answered. "The only thing missing is the flash pan." She pointed towards the barrel. "They bored the barrels and rifled them."

Joseph looked at the musket. "You only have one shot."

"That is all you need," Catherine laughed. "If you can see it, you can hit it. The round is .69 calibers. It does not matter what you hit. They are deadly at fifty yards!"

"They had less than three hundred. They did not have enough rifles," Joseph said slowly. He looked southeast towards the city of Washington. "They did not have enough rifles and they would have lost." He paused. "They would have lost."

Catherine became angry with Joseph. She had known him for four years and this was the first time he seemed negative. This was the first time, in four years, she heard him make a negative comment. "You of all people should understand the sacrifice these people made!" she yelled. "Guns were expensive in the year 1814 and difficult to obtain. The Sons of Liberty donated their guns. Without their guns they were helpless. They were prepared to sacrifice themselves for a greater good. The Sons of Liberty did not give up and we did not give up! Do not discount their spirit! Do not discount their patriotism and their love for country! I disagree, they would have won!"

Joseph raised his eyebrows. Catherine's voice was filled with fire. She was holding a flintlock rifle in her left hand and three leather pouches were across her chest. He looked at the flintlock rifle Catherine was holding. Her rifle looked different from the one he held. It looked different; it looked newer and better preserved.

"1766 French musket," Catherine said. "It belonged to Joshua Meadows one of my distant relatives."

Joseph looked surprised. "He was in the War of 1812?"

Catherine smiled proudly. "Joshua was only sixteen years old when he heard the call to arms. He was one of the defenders of Fort McHenry. He and many others defended the fort September 13th through the 14th in the year 1814."

"Really?" Joseph asked excited. "Your relative Joshua defended Fort McHenry?"

Catherine began to sing. "Oh! thus be it ever, when freemen shall stand Between their loved home and the war's desolation! Blest with victory and peace, may the heav'n rescued land Praise the Power that hath made and preserved us a nation. Then conquer we must, when our cause it is just, And this be our motto: "In God is our trust." And the Star-Spangled Banner in triumph shall wave O'er the land of the free and the home of the brave!"

Joseph and Audrey laughed and clapped.

Catherine smiled. "Joshua was one of the people who hid the original cache." She held his gun sideward with a sly smile on her face. "How do you think my father and his friends knew where to find it? The coordinates are scratched into the barrel near the breech."

Joseph laughed as he looked at Catherine. She was wearing oversized denim pants and a denim shirt. On her head was an old black hat. *Her father's?* Attached to her waist was a gun holster. She was wearing her father's gun belt and carrying her father's gun.

Joseph looked at the gun belt and frowned.

Catherine smiled. She held Joshua's flintlock rifle upward in her left hand and removed her father's gun from his holster with her right hand. She pointed at her clothing and the two guns. "Joshua and my father could not be here…today… with us." She lowered her head. "If they had not done what they did…we would not be here!" She raised her head and smiled proudly. "It's only fitting. Don't you think?"

Joseph nodded his head. "It is very fitting indeed. I am sure they are both very proud of you."

Catherine smiled.

"They work?" he asked as he looked at the rifle.

"Yes sir!" Catherine answered. "They are deadly at fifty yards!"

Joseph looked carefully at the flintlock rifle in his hands. "Pass them out!" he ordered.

"Already taken care of," Catherine said. She pointed towards the front of the transport. "It was Hammond Burke's idea."

Joseph nodded his head in approval as he looked at Audrey's leg. "Can you make it?"

"Of course," Audrey answered. "It is only two miles." She looked southeast. "When we meet up, I will ride with the others."

The three laughed as they moved into position to join the large numbers of S.A.A.G. patriots.

"Forward!" Joseph yelled.

The large contingent of members began to move forward. Hammond Burke held a pole with the flag of the United States that once flew over the nation's Capitol in the year 1812. The flag had fifteen white stars on a field of blue and fifteen alternating stripes of red and white. The stars and stripes represented fifteen states. The flag was well preserved but torn and damaged from war. This flag was hidden by the Sons of Liberty in the year 1814 and preserved in the year 1986.

Beside the 1812 flag one S.A.A.G. member, Carol Lang, held a pole with a flag of the United States. The flag was perfectly preserved and hidden by the Sons of Liberty in the year 1986. This flag had fifty white stars on a field of blue and thirteen alternating stripes of red and white. Each star represented a state and each stripe represented one of the original thirteen colonies.

Joseph, Audrey and Catherine were among the large numbers of S.A.A.G. members who followed the flag bearers. They were among a small number of members who held flintlock rifles and flintlock pistols. Around their chests they carried leather pouches filled with powder, flints and round lead balls. The small number of members was followed by larger numbers of members who held modern-day guns: pistols, rifles, shotguns and Chicago pianos.

The people in the crowd cheered as the Sons of Liberty began to move southeast, following the large numbers of S.A.A.G. members towards the nation's Capitol.

As the group slowly marched forward, Joseph looked backward. All he could see was dust. The month of June had been hot and dry soil covered the roads. All he could see was a large cloud of dust.

Hammond Burke was bearing the flag of 1812 and he began to sing. "O say can you see, by the dawns early light?"

Carol Lang was bearing the flag of 1986 and she began to sing with Hammond. "What so proudly we hailed at the twilight's last gleaming?"

Many voices began to sing with Hammond and Carol.

"Whose broad stripes and bright stars thru the perilous fight,
O'er the ramparts we watched were so gallantly streaming?
And the rocket's red glare, the bombs bursting in air,
Gave proof through the night that our flag was still there.
Oh, say does that Star-Spangled Banner yet wave
O'er the land of the free and the home of the brave?"

"On the shore, dimly seen through the mists of the deep,

Where the foe's haughty host in dread silence reposes,
What is that which the breeze, o'er the towering steep,
As it fitfully blows, half conceals, half discloses?
Now it catches the gleam of the morning's first beam,
In full glory reflected now shines in the stream:
'Tis the Star-Spangled Banner! Oh long May it wave
O'er the land of the free and the home of the brave!"

"And where is that band who so vauntingly swore
That the havoc of war and the battle's confusion,
A home and a country should leave us no more!
Their blood has washed out their foul footsteps' pollution.
No refuge could save the hireling and slave
From the terror of flight, or the gloom of the grave:
And the Star-Spangled Banner in triumph doth wave
O'er the land of the free and the home of the brave!"

"Oh! thus be it ever, when freemen shall stand
Between their loved home and the war's desolation!
Blest with victory and peace, may the heav'n rescued Land
Praise the Power that hath made and preserved us a nation.
Then conquer we must, when our cause it is just,
And this be our motto: "In God is our trust."
And the Star-Spangled Banner in triumph shall wave
O'er the land of the free and the home of the brave!"

Many cheers erupted.

Joseph Victorio did not sing with the others. He continued to march forward and looked backward. Joseph smiled as he was filled with pride.

"O beautiful for spacious skies," Joseph began to sing loudly.

"For amber waves of grain," thousands of voices joined and mixed with his.

"For purple mountain majesties
Above the fruited plain!
America! America!
God shed his grace on thee
And crown thy good with brotherhood
From sea to shining sea!"

"O beautiful for pilgrim feet
Whose stern impassioned stress
A thoroughfare of freedom beat
Across the wilderness!
America! America!
God mend thine every flaw,
Confirm thy soul in self-control,
Thy liberty in law!"

"O beautiful for heroes proved
In liberating strife.
Who more than self their country loved
And mercy more than life!
America! America!
May God thy gold refine
Till all success be nobleness
And every gain divine!"

"O beautiful for patriot dream
That sees beyond the years
Thine alabaster cities gleam
Undimmed by human tears!

America! America!
God shed his grace on thee
And crown thy good with brotherhood
From sea to shining sea!"

"O beautiful for pilgrims feet,
Whose stem impassioned stress
A thoroughfare for freedom beat
Across the wilderness!
America! America!
God shed his grace on thee
Till paths be wrought through
wilds of thought
By pilgrim foot and knee!"

"O beautiful for glory-tale
Of liberating strife
When once and twice,
for man's avail
Men lavished precious life!
America! America!
God shed his grace on thee
Till selfish gain no longer stain
The banner of the free!"

There were no cheers.

The people following the flag bearers were of different ages, cultures and race. The people sang the two songs in English and several stanzas were sung in *their* native language. The voices singing were mixed in many different languages: Spanish, English, French, Dutch, Cherokee, Navaho, Celtic, German, Russian, Italian, Amharic, Swahili, Somali, Tagalog, Tahitian, Hindi, Chinese, Japanese and several languages Joseph had never heard. The people had many differences but the events of the last four years brought them together, as one country and one nation.

The people marched slowly forward, toward the city of Washington D.C., silent and reverent. They did not cheer after singing the last stanza. The two songs reminded them of the enormous task that lay before them - rebuilding their government and their country.

Joseph Victorio was filled with pride, much pride. As he marched forward and looked backward, all he could see was a large cloud of dust. In the dust were not people but Americans.

Hundreds of thousands of Americans followed the two flags, the symbol of their country. Joseph issued a call to arms for the final push forward to reclaim their government in the name of the people, all of the people, and place their elected representatives in power.

The American people answered the call to arms to free their country. They came from every parish, hamlet, town, city and state. In their hands they carried what weapons they could locate: rakes, hoes and shovels taken from their gardens; limbs taken from the branches of trees and stone taken from the fields. Captured military transports repainted in the colors of red, white and blue; carried the ill and disabled.

The Americans marching forward were filled with pride, much pride; pride in their country and pride in themselves. For four years America cried out for help and the Sons of Liberty answered her plea. They marched forward, not as many but as one, to answer their country's cry of help for unity – No one is free until everyone is free! Put aside your differences and stand together as one!

They marched forward, together, with one single goal –

LIBERTY AND FREEDOM FOR ALL!

Epilogue

Wednesday July 4, 2046, the Government of the United States of America was reclaimed in the name of the people, all of the people; as the elected officials took their respective positions. Their first official act was to lower the flag of the United States Senate from the flagpole atop the nation's Capitol and raise the flag of the United States of America in its place; the flags hidden by the Sons of Liberty in the years 1814 and 1986. Their second official act was to abolish the Department of Harvesting. The nation began to slowly rebuild and return to the ideals and values as originally enacted in the year 1776; all men are created equal.

Thirteen statues to commemorate the event were placed on the Capitol grounds. The statues were of people; common, ordinary people. Four statues were of men and women, two as groups and two as individuals. Three statues were of families; women and men holding infant children. Two statues were of older children, alone, and two statues were of older children with their parents. Two statues were of older and younger children, brothers and sisters; holding hands and standing together with their grandparents.

Thirteen statues were erected to commemorate the events of that day and represented the number of the original thirteen colonies. The faces and clothing of the statues were muddled, to not identify one single person or one single group; muddled to identify every person and every group.

A simple sentence and date was placed on each statue.

THE SONS OF LIBERTY
WEDNESDAY JULY 4, 2046

Definition

lemon (le-mon)
noun.

1. Citrus fruit of the genus lemon.
2. Defective American manufactured automobile.
3. Defective homosapien (a person who has no conscious or guilt).
4. Cecil Marvin Morris - Appointed Speaker of the United States Senate (2024); the first Supreme Ruler of the United States of America (2024 – 2042).
5. Nathan Lewis James – Appointed Speaker of the United States Senate (2042); the second and last Supreme Ruler of the United States of America (2042 – 2046).

pa·tri·ot, pa·tri·ots
noun.

1. Defenders of the United States' Constitution.
2. A strong support, protection in danger (bulwark).
3. Legendary soldier(s) of the First American Revolution (1776 - 1781).
4. Legendary soldier(s) of the Second American Revolution (2042 - 2046).
5. The Sons of Liberty (1776), (1814), (1986), (2046); (a misnomer as all four groups, in all four time periods, had members who were male and female).

S.A.A.G. - saah·ag (SAAG)
noun.

1. **S**eniors **A**rmed **A**gainst **G**overnment mandated population control.
2. A group of people who refuse to be harvested.
3. Person(s) who harvest(s) (kill) a harvester.
4. To harvest (kill) with conscious, without regret and/or remorse to protect yourself and others.
5. Bulwark of the weak, ill and defenseless.

sup-pli-ca-tion
noun.

1. A entreat (urgent).
2. To ask humbly.
3. To pray to God humbly and earnestly.

REFERENCES

America the Beautiful. Words: Katherine Lee Bates, 1893. Revised: 1895, 1904 and 1913.
Melody: Simon Augustus Ward, 1882 (also titled *Materna*).

The Star-Spangled Banner. Words: Francis Scott Key, 1814.
Tune: *Anacreon in Heaven,* John Stafford Smith, 1771.

www.ingramcontent.com/pod-product-compliance
Lightning Source LLC
Chambersburg PA
CBHW030413310726
48979CB00002B/391

* 9 7 8 0 9 7 4 8 8 7 0 5 0 *